KODIAK
NOBLEMAN
AND THE BULL RIDER MYSTERY

DANIELLE RENEE WALLACE

Edited by Nickolas S. Wallace

To Dad, Mom, Nick, and Ethan (again):

Dad, thank you so much for the time you spent helping me out on this book, and thank you for being an awesome father! I'm very lucky. Thanks for your encouragement and ideas for this series.

Thanks, Mom, for spending time to read my book; I'm glad you liked it so much. And thank you for working hard at all your housewife stuff! I love you very much.

Hey, Nick, you work hard as my editor, and I love reading your funny comments! But of course, you already knew that, didn't you? Having my brother be the editor is definitely a perk. Thanks so much for it.

Ethan, I appreciate you reading the first book in this series (even if it did take you a while to start)! Thanks, my bro. You're really great, and I like gaming with you and Nick.

In loving memory of Mocha

August 30, 2007—August 18, 2019

TABLE OF CONTENTS

The Unexpected Uncle

Chapter 1

My life began to take an interesting turn on a sunny day during an early May. School was almost out, and summer was on the way. It was a Thursday after school, and I had waved goodbye to my two best friends, Felicia Blackwood and Lydia Arlington, calling out "see ya tomorrow!" Then I turned away and walked by myself to the ranch I call home.

I was battling homework as well as chores at the time, and both tasks were giving me a challenge.

Seven new foals had been born just a month earlier, and that had obviously been keeping me busy, not to mention I was helping my father and older brother, Ryker, build another stable. Math was making me miserable, and although Fay's—Felicia's—mother, who was teaching us at school temporarily, was a wonderful teacher, even she was having trouble helping me understand arithmetic. Math seems, to me, like rocket science. Lydia—or as I more often call her, Lia— and Fay study with me, which helps, but math is still confusing to me.

To add to everything else, Trevin Aragon, one of the rudest boys in all of sixth grade, hadn't ceased to constantly make fun of my every mistake in class. Like Fay, he is an extremely intelligent person when it comes to school, but unlike her, he is a bully.

But anyway, I had walked home from school that day putting aside those troubles. It was almost summer vacation!

Once I reached home, I only took a minute to walk into the house, drop off all my school stuff at the entryway, and head outside through the backdoor. However, once I was about to leave, I heard Mom talking in the kitchen.

Curious, I poked my head in and saw my mother on the phone. She saw me and waved a little, so I grinned and waved back. I wanted to know who she was on the phone with. At the same time, however, I knew better than to interrupt, so I decided to just head outside, like my original plan had been.

As soon as I opened the door and stepped out, my corgi, named Gopher, instantly came to see me. My family has two other dogs—Arrow, who is an Australian cattle dog, and Blue, who is a collie.

I picked Gopher up and took in the sight of my family's peaceful ranch. Sighing contently, I gazed at our wheat field. We specialize in a unique kind of wheat—einkorn—which is an ancient grain. My bedroom window faces the wheat field, and I love to look out my window at it in the mornings.

"Enjoying the scenery, Cross Eyes?"

I pulled my eyes away from the field and turned my head to the voice. I had been a little startled and almost jumped.

"I guess I didn't hear you come out, Pitchfork," I replied, slightly sheepish.

Pitchfork is the nickname I gave my older brother, Ryker, because he's scrawny but strong. Ryker's older than I am by about four years, and he's my only sibling.

Ryker nodded. "I just got home."

Ryker went to school at Beaver City because Wilsonville didn't have a school for his grade. I would be going to Beaver City too for seventh grade. I had mixed feelings about it, though.

"Well," Ryker said, plopping his cowboy hat on his head atop his dark-brown hair, "Dad wanted us to water the garden today."

I nodded. "I wonder where Dad is, anyway."

"Probably working on the new stable."

I headed toward the garden, grabbing a hoe on my way. We also had some weeding to do.

"Did you hear Mom on the phone?" I asked.

"Yeah."

"I wonder who she was talking to."

Ryker grabbed a hose and looked over at me. "Beats me. I reckon she'll tell us if it's anything important."

"I guess so," I replied, concentrating on a particularly stubborn weed.

"How was school?" Ryker asked, trying to strike up a different conversation.

I remembered my could-be-way-better grade in math but then also remembered how I totally aced art, *and* that a toad got into the cafeteria, which sent the whole school into chaos, with over three fourths of the population of girls shrieking or trying to keep their feet off the ground. Nearly all of the boys were completely thrilled at the sight of the creature as it hopped across the cafeteria and down the hallway. *That* had certainly made the day exciting!

"Where should I start?" I replied, smirking.

* * *

Later on, I was still outside working on the day's chores. The sun beat down with what seemed no mercy, and I couldn't get the thought of lemonade out of my head.

Pitchfork and I were currently watering the tomato and pepper plants. We were almost done with the garden.

"I sure would like some snickerdoodles and lemonade, wouldn't you?" I asked my older brother.

Ryker laughed and agreed.

"I've got to work today, though!" I chirped. "I'm meeting up with Lia and Fay at the bus tomorrow."

"Oh?" asked Ryker. "What's the occasion?"

I laughed. "Homework—and hanging out."

The school bus is abandoned—it has been for years—and it's in an alleyway here in Wilsonville. Lydia's mother was the first one to find it, before her passing. Then, one day, Lydia stumbled upon the bus. The bus is full of books because a long time ago, our school was robbed, and for some reason, the robbers filled the school bus with books. They weren't academic books, for the most part, anyway. They were mainly books of fiction. I'm not sure where they came from, though.

The bus is a hangout spot for me and my friends, and we often meet up at it.

"Good luck on the homework, Cross Eyes," Ryker told me with a slight smirk.

I laughed a little and pushed my strawberry-blond bangs away from my eyes. "Thanks. I have the secret weapon, though."

"Let me guess—your friends?" Ryker asked, watering the squash.

"Yup!" I replied, drizzling some water from my hose onto my head, trying to cool off. "Besides, Fay actually *loves* math. Weird, right?"

My older brother laughed a little. "Kind of. I

wouldn't say I *love* math, but it's okay."

"I guess so," I replied. "But I don't think math loves *me.*"

"Practice, and math will love you," Ryker answered me wisely.

I couldn't help but smile a little. "Well, it's not that I don't *try* to do well at math. I really do try."

Ryker nodded. "I know. Don't worry, though. Besides, aren't you getting better at history? That's something to be glad about."

"Yeah, you're right!" I replied, feeling a bit of relief. "I love the way Mrs. Blackwood teaches it."

I hadn't been doing as well in history until a couple months ago, when Fay's mother started to teach us at school.

"You know what else is something to be glad about?" Ryker asked.

"What?"

"Mom said we could have the last snickerdoodles!"

And before I could even reply, my older brother was dashing toward the house.

"Hey, wait for me!" I yelled, throwing my hose to the nearest tree and darting after him.

* * *

A little while later, we finished the chores. Normally, I would've been working on homework afterward, but I was going to do that tomorrow, when I went to the bus.

So instead, I was laying on my bed, working on

my latest drawing. I love spending time in my bedroom. The wooden floor is a dark brown color, with a cowhide run in the center, and the walls are white. I have bronze horseshoe decorations hung up, and I even have a horseshoe alarm clock on my nightstand. Ryker actually gave me the alarm clock for my birthday when I turned ten. It used to be his.

My bed has a quilt and a wooden bedframe, and on my wall is a horse calendar and a horse painting that I painted myself about a year ago. An antler chandelier hangs on my ceiling, like most of the rooms in the house.

I love the western feel my room has!

Anyway, I was drawing a boy walking on railroad tracks—just an idea that popped into my head while I was in math class. The railroad tracks eventually lead to a wheat field—an idea that popped into my head during history. Mrs. Blackwood has gotten after me a few times because I've ended up doodling on test papers and such. I've also been called on to answer a question when I'm daydreaming, which is awkward, to say the least.

I have been trying to pay better attention, though. Lia's actually kicked me in the ankle a few times during history, when I've started to space out. Believe it or not, it helps!

I was just working on the finishing touches of my drawing when I heard a familiar voice call out, "Ryker, Cody, time for dinner!"

And then I heard my older brother shout,

"Coming, Mom!"

I grinned, set down my artwork, and thumped down the stairs.

* * *

"Pass the coleslaw, Pitchfork," I said, breaking the silence at the dinner table. Something seemed off that night. Dad and Mom didn't say much, and I kind of wanted to ask what was up, but my gut instinct said to remain silent on the matter.

They'll tell me if it's anything they think I should know, I reassured myself.

Ryker turned to me, and I could tell he was also curious. I gave him a small half-smile in return.

I looked down at my plate. Silence seemed to fill the whole house—and it wasn't just any silence. It was one of those long, uncomfortable, silences.

Part of me was just dying to say something. At the same time, I felt that I couldn't really say anything at all.

I noticed Dad and Mom exchanged glances.

Mom cleared her throat a little. She gave my brother and me one of her gentle smiles. "Boys, your father and I have something to tell you."

Finally!

"What is it?" Ryker asked, tilting his head slightly to one side. I just looked at my parents with an inquisitive expression.

Dad cleared his throat a little. "I need to go to Texas—for two weeks."

"Why?" Ryker and I instantly burst out in

8

unison.

Mom sighed. "You remember Mr. Ellet, right?"

I nodded. "I think so."

"Didn't he used to live here before moving to Texas?" Ryker asked.

Mom nodded. "That's right."

Dad sighed. "Well, he called today and said that he's selling some of his horses—including a very good one, a Thoroughbred."

"Why can't you just buy it somewhere else—someplace closer?" asked Ryker.

"Well, Mr. Ellet's a good friend of mine, and he needs my help. You see, his wife is sick, and he needs the money."

"When do you leave?" I asked.

"Tuesday morning."

I frowned. "Can I come with you?"

"You know you have school, Cody," Dad replied, and I knew he was right. I could tell he felt bad about having to leave, though.

That was the answer I was expecting, but I couldn't help but sigh.

* * *

The next morning, the whole house was quiet. I soundlessly made my way down the stairs and into the kitchen. Flipping on the light switch, I opened the fridge, pulling out milk, eggs, and blueberries. Then I went to the pantry and pulled out some other ingredients. Grabbing a crisp, white apron, I tied it on.

I was totally in the mood for my infamous blueberry pancakes. They had chocolate, as well as some other secrets, even though they already had blueberries. I've been making them for years—probably since I was seven

I opened the backyard door, letting Blue, Arrow, and Gopher in for some company. They wagged their tails in response.

Dumping various things in a bowl, I hummed happily out of tune to myself. Currently, I was trying to push the thought of Dad leaving from my mind. However, I was left alone to my own thoughts in my family's quiet house.

Come on, Cody! I told myself, feeling a little silly for my overreaction. *Cheer up. It's only two weeks; you'll survive.*

"I'll still be with Mom and Ryker—and Lia and Fay, too!" I said to myself aloud, cracking an egg into the bowl. "Dad won't be away forever, only for a little while."

* * *

After breakfast, I was in the wheat field. I loved being here. Maybe it was something about the air or the comforting texture of the wheat beneath my fingers. There wasn't another place on the planet I'd rather live than in Wilsonville, Nebraska; it's home.

I took a deep breath of the clean air and closed my eyes.

For once, I let the previous pressure I had been having over everything slip away, from grades to chores to Dad leaving.

I smiled, wishing the moment could last forever. However, before I knew it, I suddenly heard Mom shout, "Cody!"

Mom was standing in the doorway and waved for me to come over.

I quickly hurried away from the wheat field and to the house instead.

The first person I saw once I reached the house was Ryker, and I followed him into the kitchen, where both Dad and Mom were.

"What's up?" I asked, taking a seat on the counter.

I noticed Mom had the phone in her hand, so I assumed someone must have called. I instantly felt a little excited, wondering who the caller could have been. We didn't get phone calls very often unless Fay's family, Lia, or Lia's grandmother called.

"My younger brother, Colton, is coming for a visit."

I was shocked and silent.

"Wait... You have a brother named Colton, Mom?" I asked. I was feeling even more excited now. An uncle I never even knew I had was coming to visit *us!*

He's probably so cool! Suppose he's like a real cowboy. I wonder if he's been in all kinds of rodeos—maybe he's even a bull rider!

Ryker looked interested, too. "I... think I might remember him—from a long time ago."

Dad nodded. "That's right. He visited us years ago."

I tilted my head to the side a little. "Was I born yet?"

Mom smiled. "You were just a baby."

Well, that certainly explained why I didn't remember him. It was weird to never even know I had an uncle named Colton.

"When's he coming?" I asked excitedly.

"Monday evening," Mom replied, and then she hesitated. "And... I was thinking that maybe I should go with your father to Texas."

Ryker's eyes widened, and I felt mine do the same. Ryker quickly said, "If you're both leaving on Tuesday, that means you'll only have a little time to catch up—after over a decade!"

Dad nodded with a sad smile. "I told Heather she shouldn't worry about me, but you know how your mother is."

"Well," Mom began, "Colton said he isn't sure how long he'll be staying in Wilsonville. He thinks it will probably be a while, though. We'll still have time to catch up, hopefully."

"So now you're *both* leaving?" I asked disappointedly.

"I'm afraid so," my father said. He smiled a little, though, and added, "But I suppose you boys and Colton can all stay here and hang out together."

That made me perk up a little more, and with a short laugh, I said, "Ryker and I will have him all to ourselves."

Ryker smirked. "How old is Uncle Colton, anyway?"

"He's thirty-four," Mom replied.

So cool! I thought. *I can't wait to tell Fay and Lia all about him!*

"Where does he live?" I asked.

"North Dakota."

That isn't too far away, so how come I only met him when I was a baby?

Ryker seemed to read my thoughts. "How come it's been so long since we've seen him if he's only a couple states away?"

Mom shrugged. "He's younger than me by almost a decade, and traveling can be expensive."

"But we'll finally get to catch up now!" I said cheerfully.

I began to think about the fun things I could do with my uncle, such as eating snickerdoodles, introducing him to my friends, horseback riding every day—maybe he would even stay during the Fourth of July, and we could have a fireworks show!

I felt a feeling of excitement bubble up in me. There were so many thoughts swirling around in my mind. I wondered what Uncle Colton was like.

I beamed.

This summer is going to be amazing.

CAFFEINE

Chapter 2

"Hey, I'm finally here!" I shouted as the abandoned bus came into view. I parked my bike but was perplexed to see my friends had not arrived yet. So much had happened since I last saw them, and I was bubbling over with excitement to tell them everything!

Usually, I'm the one who's late. I wonder what's up with the girls.

Sometimes it is a little weird—awkward even—having both your best friends be females. I've definitely been teased about it, but I'm used to constant teasing about what seems like *everything*.

Yes, people, I'm aware I'm not the most intelligent person in school, and *yes,* I know I don't have a thousand friends.

I decided to look for a good book in the bus while I waited, and I ended up choosing a rather interesting novel about horses.

A small amount of time passed, but I looked up from the book when I heard the familiar sound of bicycle wheels. I grinned and waved as Fay and Lia pulled up.

Both girls parked their bikes and waved back.

"You beat us," Lydia said with a grin.

Felicia heaved a sigh. "I never thought I'd see the day."

"Trust me, neither did I," I replied, adding with a smirk, "However, I would not by any means think *you* would be late! Not ever!"

Felicia playfully rolled her blue eyes and smiled.

Lydia laughed "Well, *I'm* only late because I helped Grandmother with the dishes."

I nodded. Lia lives with her grandmother; she has ever since Mr. and Mrs. Arlington passed.

"Valid reason," I stated. "But guys, I've got so much to tell you!"

"Well, I'm not a 'guy,' Cody," Fay clarified with a smirk, "but what's happened since we saw you last?"

"Yeah," Lia agreed, "we saw you, like, less than

twenty-four hours ago."

"Well," I replied, "quite a bit."

Lydia tilted her head in curiosity. "Fill us in?"

"Totally."

* * *

"Whoa," Felicia breathed. "So now your uncle is coming over on Monday, but your parents are leaving on Tuesday?"

I nodded. "Yup. Oh, and to make matters crazier, we haven't even told Uriah yet!"

Purposely being a bit overdramatic, Lydia said, "Good luck, Code."

I playfully rolled my eyes.

Uriah was a man in his mid-twenties who moved to Wilsonville a few months ago. He was going to marry a teacher the girls and I used to have, but that's a different story. Anyway, my father hired him to help us out with things on the ranch. Uriah was taking a vacation upstate that week, though, so he hadn't been filled in.

We all talked some more about my uncle until Fay held up her stack of books. "History test. Studying needs to be done."

"Ugh," I moaned.

Lia sighed, seeing the topic of study less interesting than news of my new visitor.

"There's a math test, too," she said.

"No...!" I wailed.

"Well, we can hang out after we study some," replied Lydia.

"And school's almost out, remember?" Fay added, trying to cheer everyone up despite mentioning something she personally didn't like to think about.

"Yeah." I replied and then grinned some. "Which means I'll have more free time to bake snickerdoodles!"

Fay and Lia both laughed.

"So," Felicia began, "study at my house?"

Lydia and I nodded, and the three of us headed to Fay's.

* * *

A couple of hours later, we had done much studying, and my head felt like it was about to explode. However, the girls had both worked hard to help make math much clearer than it had been for me. History would still need some work done for my comprehension, but I trusted we could work that out.

The girls and I were in the Blackwoods' kitchen, pigging out—well, actually, I was the only one pigging out—on leftover cupcakes. You see, Lydia had spent the night at Fay's yesterday, and they decided to bake cupcakes, so now they had about fifteen cupcakes sitting around. Well, there certainly wouldn't be fifteen there for long, thanks to me, of course.

"Mmm…" I mumbled, savoring the flavor of something I couldn't quite place. "Hey Fay, what kind of cupcake is this?"

"Coffee," she replied simply. However, I stared for a moment.

"So… were you guys up all night, then?"

Lia giggled.

"No, of course not!" she declared.

"But," Fay added softly, "we were up pretty late, and feeling—"

"Sleep deprived," Lydia finished, waving her arms out in front of her, impersonating a zombie.

I playfully gave her a look and muttered, "Crazy girl…"

"Yeah, we went to bed at, like, twelve," Fay added.

I almost spit out the milk I was drinking. Swallowing it down, I then shouted, "At noon?"

Fay gave me a long stare. At last, she replied, "At midnight."

"Oh."

Lydia let out a long and loud yawn. "But after we went to bed, we were too awake to sleep—must have been the caffeine."

"Well, I was sleepy, for one, but you certainly weren't," Felicia replied.

I smiled. They were a funny pair of friends.

"I'm not used to that much caffeine," Lia

defended.

I raised an eyebrow.

"Just how much caffeine did you guys—I mean, girls—*have?*"

Fay was silent for a moment, mentally calculating.

"Well, there was the cup of coffee when we arrived at my house, and then the spot of tea at dinner, then another cup of coffee probably an hour or so before bed, and finally the coffee cupcakes."

If this were a movie, you would've heard crickets in the background. I had to blink after hearing that long list.

"Well, I know you frequently have coffee, Fay, but as for Lia… that's a whole different story. It's a wonder she wasn't bouncing off the walls."

"But they put mint in their coffee—which is amazing!" Lydia chirped.

"Fay, do you usually have that much coffee?" I asked.

"Well, my mom has it around all the time, but that was more caffeine than I'm used to; in fact, I think I sort of crashed from it last night. We meant to get decaffeinated coffee, but we grabbed the wrong bag—my mother was trying out this new brand—and Lia and I didn't realize it until it was too late."

"I'm probably never going to have that much caffeine at once again," Lia said, "though it was kind of fun."

I shot Fay a look.

* * *

"Thanks for letting us study at your house, Mrs. Blackwood," Lydia said politely.

Remembering my manners, I also showed my appreciation for the Blackwoods' kindness.

Fay tried to send home some of the cupcakes with Lia and me, but Lia said she had better not because she had already devoured enough caffeine for one week—or month. However, Fay did end up sending one for Lia's grandmother. As for me, I accepted Fay's kind offer, also knowing Ryker would want a cupcake.

Mrs. Blackwood, who was giving apple sauce to Fay's little sister (she was about one and a half years old), said to me: "Oh, Cody, were you saying your relative is coming to your house?"

"Yeah!" I chirped and then gushed, "He's my uncle, and I can't wait to meet him—I've never even met him before, but Ryker has. Well, actually, I have met him, but I was just a baby, so I don't remember it at all."

"Oh, which uncle is it?"

"My uncle Colton! I really can't wait to see him and—"

Mrs. Blackwood laughed a little at my excitement. "I remember Colton; he was much younger than your mother, though, and I didn't know him as well."

I nodded. "The bad news is my dad has to leave—he's going to buy a Thoroughbred—and my mom is going to go with him. So, sadly, they won't get nearly as long of a reunion."

"Oh no," Mrs. Blackwood replied softly. "How long will Colton be in Wilsonville?"

"Don't know yet," I responded. "I hope a long time—a *very* long time…"

Arrival and Departure

Chapter 3

Monday evening at four o'clock—that's what the date and time had been. I was practically bubbling over with excitement. All day long, from the moment school began to its last minutes, I had found myself waiting for it to be over. All day long, questions filled my mind, such as these:

Has Uncle Colton already arrived?
If he hasn't, where is he right now?
If he has, what am I missing out on?

And, of course:

Suppose he likes snickerdoodles as much as I do?

From when I woke up that morning until four o'clock that afternoon, these thoughts and others filled my mind. And such would continue to occur until my long-awaited uncle arrived.

There were also times of fear—fear I couldn't push aside—that my uncle might not like me that much.

It was a horrible thought, and I tried to push it aside the moment it first came to me. However, a worry as deep as this was not easily dismissed.

Such a thought wasn't entirely revealed in full force. It was quiet, yet nagging—inconspicuous at times, but there. It was like a gentle tugging on your sleeve or a whisper in your ear. For me, it was that anxious feeling deep down in the pit of my stomach. I would distract myself for a time, but it would always come back. And when it did come, it made concentrating on other things difficult—just like when someone is tugging on your sleeve.

In contrast, Ryker seemed entirely at ease.

I worked diligently on my homework once I had gone home—Uncle Colton hadn't arrived. I was sure it was only a matter of time until he would, though, and I made an effort to look out a window every five minutes or so.

After I finished all the assigned homework, I went outside to do all my chores, continually glancing at the dirt road. He still hadn't arrived.

Once all the chores were complete, I pulled up a chair by a window and waited for my uncle.

Then, left alone to my thoughts, I felt two emotions that were, in a way, battling inside me. One was excitement, and the other, nervousness. Both were very strong at that present moment. Rejection was a fear, but friendship a hope. I tried to focus on the hope, but at times, the gentle whisper, the tugging on the sleeve, would sneak back. Cruel thing!

I inwardly told myself to snap out of it. I would try my best to make an excellent first impression on Uncle Colton and hope he would accept his nephew's invitation to friendship.

I inhaled deeply and then let out huge a sigh of relief. Yes, I would do as I could and hope for the best; there really wasn't anything else I could do. So, with such a fear slipping from my mind for the time, I peered out the freshly washed window for what seemed ages.

* * *

Thud!

I nearly jumped out of my skin. It took a moment for me to realize what had happened. When the realization arrived, I felt what must have been a blush rise to my cheeks since Ryker had clearly seen the whole thing.

Apparently, while I was on the chair waiting for Uncle Colton, I had gotten bored and, quite frankly, fallen asleep. Well, a wooden dining room chair never did make a good bed, and I had unintentionally fallen off while sleeping! On top of all that, when I had taken my fall, my head hit one of our very large plant pots.

Ryker laughed loudly, and I felt my lips turn up into a slight smile. The sight would have obviously appeared humorous if I had seen *him* do such a thing.

I rubbed my sore head and felt relieved to see that it wasn't bleeding and that Mom's plant pot hadn't cracked. I yawned sleepily but playfully rolled my eyes at my brother, who hadn't felt it necessary to ask if I was okay.

I laughed dryly but stopped suddenly when I saw a rather old and muddy pickup pulling into our driveway. I quickly pushed my face up against the window.

"Mom! Ryker! Dad!" I exclaimed, rushing to the door and almost slipping. "He's here!"

I was extremely excited, so it was hard for me even to grab the doorknob and turn it—I kept on missing, and my hand was shaking, you see—but once I finally got that done, I flung the door open and scurried outside.

"Uncle Colton!" I cheered a couple times, waving.

He stepped out of his muddy truck, which was gray-colored.

Uncle Colton wore a black, western hat that was a little dusty looking; a blue and white gingham shirt; light-blue jeans; and a pair of boots that looked as if they had undoubtedly been worn out. Like Ryker, his eyes were dark blue, and his hair was dark brown.

I smiled a little to myself. He looked just like a real cowboy.

Maybe that's where Ryker got his brown hair and blue eyes.

My brother appeared outside, and Dad and Mom as well.

"Colton!" Mom delightfully exclaimed and gave her younger brother a giant hug. "I'm so glad to see you."

Dad shook Uncle Colton's hand and asked him how his trip was. Ryker went over to our uncle next, and I followed behind him. My mind felt blank; I couldn't think of what I should say.

However, I recovered in time and beamed.

"I'm so glad to meet you, Uncle Colton," I chirped. Then I gushed for a couple minutes about how I was just bubbling over with excitement and how I couldn't wait to show him everything—

especially my horse, Nightfall.

Uncle Colton looked me over thoughtfully. He stared, which started to make me a little uncomfortable. At last, he said, "You must be... um..."

His voice died away, and I could tell he was thinking deeply. I waited.

He hesitated a little and then said, "You're Cody?"

I beamed. "Yeah! My real name's Kodiak, but I get called Cody a *lot*—which is completely fine, by the way."

A brief look of realization spread over his face. "I remember you... but you were a baby last time I saw ya. You're how old?"

"Twelve," I replied cheerfully. "But I'm going to be thirteen on the twenty-sixth of July!"

Uncle Colton asked Ryker how old he was, to which he promptly replied, "Sixteen."

Our uncle was surprised at how fast time flew.

Mom beckoned Uncle Colton to come inside, and so we all filed in.

I grinned deeply.

This is going to be great!

* * *

"Lost my farm. Had to sell near everything."

I stared, my jaw dropping.

We were all sitting on the leather couches in the

living room, and Uncle Colton was telling us about his current dilemma.

"Oh, that's awful," Mom quietly exclaimed.

"How did it happen?" Dad asked.

Uncle Colton sighed. "Locusts came. Devoured my fields. Lost a lot of money that way. And hail ruined whatever was left and destroyed my barn."

Ryker tilted his head. "Didn't you have insurance?"

Uncle Colton shook his head soberly. "Nope."

"Why'd you come to Wilsonville, though?" I asked innocently.

"Sold all my stock and wanted to start fresh."

"Start fresh in Wilsonville?" I asked.

"Maybe. Hoping I could do some work here first. If I could make some money... I might be able to buy a farm later."

"So, you wanted to get a job at our ranch?" Dad asked.

Colton gave one nod.

Dad was silent for a moment, thinking.

I was holding my breath, intensely wanting Dad to hire Uncle Colton. Then, who knows how long he'd be around!

Please, please, please.

Dad looked at Mom, who gave a small, encouraging nod.

Clearing his throat, Dad said, "Well, we do have

quite a bit of work going on. It's been keeping the boys and me busy. We could use a little extra help. And with Uriah on vacation…"

I exhaled.

Yes! This is really happening.

Uncle Colton looked slightly perplexed. "Uriah?"

"Yeah," Dad said. "He's someone else I hired— real nice guy."

Heartily, I nodded in agreement.

"I like Uriah a lot!" I shouted a little too loudly.

Dad began discussing wages with Uncle Colton, and Ryker and I exchanged happy glances.

* * *

Later, salaries had been discussed and agreed upon.

I was awake for a long time that night, my mind too full to sleep. At first, it wasn't so fun, and then, after a while, it was very irritating. Unable to doze, I sighed in aggravation. Time seemed to pass like a snail crossing a six-lane road.

I imagine everyone's had a night like that at some point. And if they haven't, they will in time should they sleep enough nights.

Oh, I certainly tossed and turned. I ended up switching around so that my feet were on my pillow and my head on the end of the bed. I tried to fall asleep on my stomach; that didn't work.

I stretched out on my back and huffed, making my strawberry-blond bangs flutter up a bit. I kicked my quilt completely off my bed, which ended up only frustrating me further. I buried my face in my pillow, and my face scrunched up in annoyance.

When one is so excited, it is very hard to fall asleep, even if you'd like to very much.

I dreaded the sight of my horseshoe alarm clock.

However, by the time I finally got out of bed and put the quilt back on securely, I yawned. I fluffed up the pillow and got resituated underneath the covers. It was only a matter of time until one of my arms was dangling over the bedframe and I was out like a light.

* * *

When dawn came, I wasn't in the mood to leave the warm covers and ended up sleeping through my alarm. Once I finally did wake up and saw that I had clearly slept an extra half an hour, I still felt like sleeping for as long as my family would let me. But then, of course, the fantastic smell of pancakes made its way up the stairs, and I could faintly hear talking which was most likely coming from the kitchen.

Yawning loudly, I got out of bed, having to laugh a little at my very messed-up hair.

It wasn't long until I felt much more awake and cheerfully rushed down the stairs.

I was the last person in the kitchen, but I put

myself to use, seasoning the eggs. Mom always loves it when I help her in the kitchen, and it's something I enjoy as well.

My tardiness in coming down had received a teasing from Ryker, and he didn't cease to use my familiar nickname, Cross Eyes. I found myself smirking, briefly recalling the event that had earned me such a title, but then turned back to culinary matters.

As the grownups talked to each other, I tried to push aside the gloominess of my parents leaving. After all, at least I'd have Uncle Colton and Ryker with me.

Speaking of those two, I couldn't help but recall how much Ryker looked like Uncle Colton when it came to hair and eye color. I briefly thought about how my hair and eyes were basically a blend of my parents' ones. (Dad has red hair and green eyes, and Mom has blonde hair and brown eyes). Ryker's hair and eyes don't resemble either of theirs, and I always wondered about that.

Pitchfork certainly shared some of his appearance with my uncle.

Funny how things work out like that.

* * *

"And remember to turn off the stove after using it in the mornings, and—"

"—put up all the ingredients," I finished for my

mother with a little bit of a smirk. "I know, Mom; I won't forget."

"And remember to make sure the dishwasher is actually clean before you take out all the dishes."

"Of course I will."

Mom gave me a small smile and let out a soft sigh. "You're right. You're twelve, not five."

"I'm almost thirteen," I reminded her cheerfully.

"Yeah," Ryker joined in, smirking teasingly. "It's not like Cross Eyes is going to burn the whole house down—at least not when I'm here to stop him, anyway."

I giggled.

Mom gave one nod and said, "I'm being silly, I suppose, for being so worried. But don't forget to—"

"Heather," Dad began, "we're already running late."

Again, Mom nodded, and then there was much exchanging of hugs.

Soon, Dad and Mom were in the truck driving off, pulling the horse trailer behind, and we were shouting goodbyes to them. We stood and waited, waving until they were out of sight. I felt a little glum.

However, I had school, so that was certainly an immediate priority—just two weeks left until summer vacation. Seeing as it was my last couple of weeks to ever go to this school and that I'd be going to Beaver City when the new school year started, I was filled with mixed emotions. That would be when I started seventh grade, and although I didn't tell the world this, I was somewhat terrified.

Gazing at the road where my parents had driven out of sight, I felt a longing for them to return. I sighed.

"Miss Dad and Mom already, Cross Eyes?"

I turned to Ryker, who was about a yard away from me. Uncle Colton had already gone inside, it appeared.

In a quiet voice, I replied, "Yes."

Ryker gave me an encouraging smile. "They'll be back soon."

I nodded but didn't say anything.

* * *

"Guess who's at my house!" I chirped excitedly to my best friends.

"Your uncle?" Lydia asked.

"Yup!"

Felicia tilted her head a little as if thinking.

"What's he like?"

"A *real* cowboy!"

We were at school, but it was currently one of the most beautiful parts of the school day—lunch. I hadn't got a chance to talk to Fay or Lia up until just now, seeing as I had been a minute or so late to school.

As we made our way to our usual table, I gushed about my relative.

"Oh, and get this," I said, slipping into a seat. "His appearance... is like... Ryker's!"

"Really?" Lia asked.

"Wait, did I hear that right?" Fay inquired, now tuning in. She previously seemed to be thinking about what we were just taught in class or something—you know how Fay is—but my surprising news apparently got her attention.

I nodded heartily in agreement and was about to continue talking about my uncle, but I fell silent when I saw Trevin Aragon approaching our table. There was a light smirk on his face, and his cold, blue eyes glittered with trouble. Seeing this, I felt a chill down my spine and a sinking feeling in my stomach. My heart quickened nervously.

I was sure that if Fay had brought a textbook or something, she would try to hide behind it.

Lia inhaled deeply, eyeing Trevin suspiciously. If she was fearful, she did an excellent job of not showing it.

Trevin was taller than me by a good four inches or so, and the way he walked with his head high up always made him seem like a tower.

"How's it going, *Cody?*"

He put added emphasis on my name in a way I wasn't fond of. Briefly, the thought that Trevin clearly meant bad news flickered through my mind.

I was silent for a moment and then replied blandly, "How can I help you?"

"I thought I'd drop by to say hello. But *how's it going?*"

I was taken aback when he sat down in an empty seat next to me. Waiting for my answer, he stared me in the face.

His gaze made me uneasy, and I broke the eye contact.

The first thought of response that came to my mind was, "Well, it was going pretty fantastic until about one minute ago," but I didn't dare say that. My throat went dry, and I quickly took a sip of water, my hand shaking a little bit.

For a moment, my mind was blank.

Trevin gave me another slight smirk before he went on to say, "Well, let's just say I couldn't help but notice your history grade."

I blushed.

"And?"

"If you'd like, maybe I could help you memorize some basic history facts."

I winced at the word *basic* and then noticed quite a few of the kids from nearby tables all looking at us. They seemed greatly interested.

Now he's made a scene...

"Um... no thanks. I-I've been studying with the

girls, and—"

Trevin, as well as some of the kids at the other tables, snickered, and I felt the blush deepening. Life isn't easy when your best friends are two girls.

"And, Ryker could help me if I needed it…"

The giggling quieted down. After all, Ryker was a respected member of society.

"Well," said Trevin, "I heard your parents are out of town."

"Who told you?" I asked, the blush fading from my cheeks.

Trevin smirked again and said, "Who says you need to know?"

Lia narrowed her eyes at Trevin, and Fay sat up a little straighter.

Trevin continued.

"Just you and your brother at your house?"

"Nah," I replied, feeling more confident.

"So *he's* there, eh?"

"Hmm…" I mumbled. "It seems news travels quickly. Yeah, my uncle's over."

Trevin stood up at last, crossing his arms over his chest.

"I've heard stuff about him."

"Like what?" I questioned.

"Rodeo stuff. But I'd suppose *you'd* already know that."

Confused, I furrowed my eyebrow.

"No?" Trevin asked and then heaved a sigh. "Well, guess I'll leave it at that. Later."

With that, he just up and left, leaving me, Fay, and Lia very confused.

Thunder

Chapter 4

Two days later, I was in my wheat field of einkorn, thinking. I ran my fingers over some of the wheat and breathed deeply. The crop was significant—the largest we had—and I loved it.

The sun was warm on my face, and a gentle breeze floated on the air. It brought me back to memories of a Fourth of July from a couple years ago, when the weather felt very much the same.

A small frown of concentration spread over my face when I recalled the lunchroom run-in that occurred just two days prior.

"He's… heard stuff about him," I muttered to

myself. "But what?"

I sighed.

So far, Trevin hadn't said anything to me since, which was fine. The day before, however, after school ended, one of his friends was walking out of the building, coming next to Fay, Lia, and me and asked me if I was going to go study with "a couple of giggling schoolgirls" for the next test. I opened my mouth to speak but then closed it. Lydia, however, calmly replied that there was nothing wrong with me studying with females, and I almost laughed when Fay invited him to come join us. He promptly turned her down and left with a scoff.

I was certainly glad to have friends like them, but there was a part of me that wished I had at least one close *guy* friend at school. Then maybe things would be a little less awkward. Still, there were always my grades, which were almost as embarrassing. That was something kids just loved to talk about. One way or another, someone discovered how one of my papers had turned out and made a huge spectacle of it. Sometimes they'd even get ahold of my paper and wave it in the air, and I was always stressed out they wouldn't hand it back. So, needless to say, I had made my best effort to shove any test papers into my backpack as soon as possible, which often meant not even glancing at the grade.

Lately, however, my grades had been going up

for the most part. There was still that history grade from two days ago, but things were getting better.

I observed the wheat field, taking in its beauty.

Who cares if Lia and Fay are girls? They've got to be some of the best friends in the world...

I gazed at wheat all around me. The field looked so golden in the evening sun. I silently felt that its color was symbolizing something.

These days are as bright as the wheat. Uncle Colton's come over and all's golden...

I was jolted out of my thoughts, however, upon hearing loud shouting. I turned to the direction of the noise and saw Uncle Colton in the corral, with one of the new horses we got.

Surprised, I widened my eyes. Dashing toward the corral, I bolted down the path of dirt through the wheat field.

"Uncle Colton!" I shouted as I approached.

"What?" he yelled back, lasso in hand.

"He—Thunder—he's new!" I panted. "You shouldn't try to—"

"Don't think I can't ride him," Uncle Colton replied, concentrating on the stallion. "I used to be a bull rider, boy!"

I was astounded.

"Wait, really?"

"Of course. Surely I can ride a horse, eh?"

He had made a point, indeed. I was about to

speak but stopped myself, interested in seeing what he'd do.

Thunder was not willing to allow Uncle Colton on top of him. He bucked and neighed, and my heart jumped when he almost kicked Uncle Colton.

I stood there, watching in a mix of terror and delight.

Uncle Colton wasn't fazed by Thunder's agitation. When the lasso skillfully landed on the horse's neck, I almost cheered.

Before I knew it, Uncle Colton was sitting on Thunder, who was still wildly bucking in protest. I was awestruck.

I counted the seconds in my head starting in the hundreds, as that's how I've always done it.

101, 102, 103, 104...

The terror was gone. Excitement replaced the void.

...109, 110, 111, 112...

Thunder was neighing loudly. I could see he was furious.

...116, 117, 118, 119...

Holding my breath, I leaned over the corral fence.

...124, 125, 126, 127...

It was almost thirty seconds. Uncle Colton was holding on tightly, and Thunder was still bucking as hard as he could.

...*130, 131, 132, 133*...

Then, Ryker came running from the house, shouting.

...*137, 138, 139, 140*...

The show going on in the corral was amazing. I beamed.

...*145, 146, 147, 148*...

"Stop! Stop this instant!" Ryker yelled.

Uncle Colton did not stop. I continued counting in my head to track his seconds of riding, ignoring my brother.

...*151, 152, 153, 154!*

At last, Thunder stopped bucking. I cheered loudly, shouting, amazed and thrilled.

Ryker wasn't shouting the same way I was.

"Stop!" he called out. His blue eyes were indignant.

Uncle Colton slid off Thunder, seeing his victory.

"That was amazing!" I shouted. "You must have lasted almost sixty seconds."

Uncle Colton smirked. "See? That was nothing like what I used to do."

Beaming, I asked Ryker, "Wasn't it the coolest thing?"

Ryker sighed heavily, putting the back of his hand to his forehead.

I beamed.

"Wasn't it awesome?" I asked enthusiastically.

Ryker glared at Uncle Colton. "I *said* you shouldn't ride him! He hurt his leg last week and doesn't like it much if even *I* ride him. He doesn't know you!"

"It's all fine," Uncle Colton responded. "He accepted me."

Ryker breathed in sharply through his nose. Turning on his heel, he crossed his arms and walked back to the farmhouse.

My eyes fell on one of Thunder's front legs.

"Is it okay?" I asked my uncle. "Thunder's leg?"

Uncle Colton went and checked. After a moment, he turned to me.

"Yeah, yeah, looks fine. Your brother's just on edge."

"Why?"

"Probably because of your parents' trip."

I nodded. "Hopefully they'll be back early."

Uncle Colton was silent for a moment, thinking.

"This is a good ranch," he muttered, somewhat to himself.

Again, I nodded. "And you're a good rider."

He briefly grinned but was silent, as if thinking again.

"Ought to start bull riding again…"

I perked up.

"And then I can go to your rodeos and watch

you. That'd be fun!"

Then we were both silent.

Looking at the gray-colored stallion and recalling the earlier events of my Uncle's ride made me remember something.

Perhaps Trevin heard about how Uncle Colton was a bull rider. Maybe Uncle Colton's famous!

* * *

The next day, Uriah arrived back from his vacation.

Introducing himself to Uncle Colton and shaking his hand, Uriah said, "I'm Uriah Harper."

"Colton Honeysett," replied my uncle.

I grinned a little at the last name. A long time ago, my own mother had been a Honeysett—Heather Honeysett. Then she married Dad and became Heather Nobleman. I have a tendency to crack a joke about how her actual last name should be Noblewoman, since she's a girl, but last names don't work like that.

"So, how long are you staying in Wilsonville?" Uriah asked my uncle.

We were outside, on the driveway.

"Not sure," Uncle Colton replied. "Hopefully for a good while."

"Hopefully," I agreed.

Uriah smiled at me. "It's good to see you again, Cody."

It was at this moment that Ryker came from the barn after finishing the watering, shook Uriah's hand, and said he was glad Uriah was back and that he hoped he had had a good vacation.

Uriah had been informed of Uncle Colton's arrival, so it was no great shock for him to see my uncle upon returning from vacation.

"How long have you been working over here?" Uncle Colton asked.

"About two months."

The two adults began to talk to each other, and I wandered off, deciding to let them get to know one another better. I headed to the house to get a snickerdoodle.

Ryker remained outside, and as I dipped my cookie in a glass of milk, I eyed a photo of my brother and me in the kitchen. It was in a nice horseshoe picture frame, and we were both considerably shorter in the photo; I think it had been taken about four years prior. Felicia and Lydia like to look at it and talk about how little Ryker and I looked, giggling like the schoolgirls they are.

I silently felt that I didn't want to grow up right away; I was okay with being twelve for a little while longer.

Besides, I thought, munching on my snickerdoodle, *once you grow up, there isn't any turning back.*

I quietly pondered about youth for a while—and then grabbed another snickerdoodle.

* * *

"What's that—a dishrag?"

Uncle Colton smirked at me, pointing to a bright-red piece of knitted cloth.

"No," I replied, feeling a little self-conscious. "It's… it's a hot pad—you know, for pots…"

Uncle Colton tilted his head. "How come it's in your room?"

"I'm not finished with it."

"Wait. You say you're *making* it?"

Embarrassed, I nodded. "Yes…"

"Who taught you to crochet?"

"It's kn-knitting," I mumbled.

"Same thing. Who taught you?"

"Ryker…"

I had been working on math in my room when Uncle Colton had come up to… Well, I wasn't really sure why he came up.

Uncle Colton's eyebrow furrowed.

"Who taught him?"

"Mom."

Uncle Colton fell silent.

I quickly put the hot pad in a shoe box which was conveniently sitting nearby. (It was free of shoes, of course.)

"It's for Mom. Don't let her know; it's a

surprise."

Uncle Colton gave a slow nod.

We were both silent, and I felt awkward.

Thankfully, Uncle Colton broke the silence.

"I like working with leather."

I tilted my head a little and beamed. "Really? That sounds so cool."

He went on to explain the stuff he enjoyed making and how he first started long ago. I listened with great interest.

"Even made the leather vest I'm wearing, see?" my uncle explained.

Wide-eyed, I had to reply, "It looks *so* cool!"

Working with leather seemed much more manly than knitting.

* * *

"He's... so cool!" I gushed.

Lia and Fay both smiled at me.

"Well," said Lydia, "I look forward to meeting him."

Fay nodded quickly. "Yes, indeed!"

We were, of course, talking about Uncle Colton.

"But when *will* we meet him?" Lia inquired.

"Hopefully soon."

I couldn't wait for my friends to meet my uncle.

"You should've seen him riding Thunder!" I added. "He lasted almost a minute."

"That horse is wild," Lydia said in

understanding.

Felicia ducked a little under her math book. "And tall..."

I laughed gleefully.

Fay was intelligent, there was no doubt about it. She could listen to Ryker talk about high school things like the Pythagorean theorem, eager to find out, even though she hadn't taken algebra yet. We were in sixth grade, after all.

"Well, he's sixteen and a half hands tall," I said.

"What about feet?"

I laughed at Fay's response. "Beats me; you do the math."

Lydia grinned. "He's certainly tall, nonetheless."

We were at Lydia's house. Her grandmother was in the kitchen cooking dinner, which smelled very good. Lia's grandmother is very cool—she's brave, is wise, *and* owns a convertible. Yes, you heard that third one right.

The doorbell rang and Lydia said she'd get it, so she left. Fay and I remained silent.

"Oh, hi, Rhys. How are you? Won't you come in?"

Rhys was another one of Ryker's nicknames, so I knew who arrived. Of course, only *I* call him Pitchfork.

I heard the door shut and Ryker greeting Lydia, asking how she was doing.

"I'm well, thank you," Lydia replied. "Anything you need?"

"Well, not really. But I thought I'd get Cody."

They both entered into the kitchen now. I noticed Ryker seemed a little tired or something.

"Hi, Mrs. Adams," said Ryker, greeting Lydia's grandmother. Her last name is Adams, as opposed to Arlington, since she's Lia's grandmother through Liliana, Lia's mother.

Felicia grinned a little. "Hello, Ryker!"

"Hi, Fay. Instructing Cody on the basics of math?"

"Hey!" I said. "What do you mean by 'basics'?"

Ryker gave me a grin, but I noted it was a rather quick one.

"Teasing. But really, Cody, we need to get back. I think it may rain soon, and the horses…"

I saw his point and nodded.

"Right. Thanks for having me over," I said, giving Lia a high-five.

I thanked Lydia's grandmother and said goodbye to Fay, then left with my older brother.

Ryker and I made our way down the sidewalks silently, each of us in thought. I found myself wondering what Dad and Mom were doing right at that moment. I thought about this for a while, until I noticed a beetle scurrying away from us on the sidewalk.

"Say, Ryker?"

"Hm?"

"Remember that time when we tried to raise beetles, and you and I forgot to feed them, so they ended up resorting to cannibalism?"

In the evening sun, I could see Ryker's cheeks turn a light dusting of pink.

"We got grounded for that one."

"Yeah, and the poor beetles…"

We were silent again. All was quiet, other than the tweeting of the birds.

* * *

Later, when we got back, Uncle Colton was nowhere to be seen outside. Ryker and I went into the house, then I got a tall glass of water, gulped it, briefly acknowledged the picture of my brother and me, and thumped up the stairs.

As I was walking through the hallway upstairs, I noted the door to my parents' room was slightly open. Recalling that it had previously been closed, I peered through the opening.

Nothing appeared to be different. I pushed the door open about midway and casually entered.

The pendulum of my parents' grandfather clock swung faithfully back and forth, and I observed the timepiece.

Who'd you see? I wondered silently. It couldn't say a thing, though. It could only make tick-tock noises, its pendulum swinging back and forth as always.

"Nothing looks out of place," I said to myself.

I glanced around the room once more and drew the conclusion that there was nothing different and nothing to be concerned about. Ending my search, I slipped out of the room, shut the door, and went to my own bedroom to grab my western hat.

Upon grabbing it, I flew down the stairs and almost bumped into Ryker in my haste.

"Hey! What's up?" he asked.

"Off to ride Nightfall!" I yelled in response.

I was about to head out of the house when I stopped and turned back to my sibling.

"Hey, Ryker, did you go in Dad and Mom's bedroom today?"

He briefly thought a moment, then shook his head. "No, why?"

"I just saw it was opened a bit today. All seems the same, though."

Without waiting for his response, I opened the door, inhaled the fresh air, and rushed to the stables.

Little did I know what I was about to discover.

The Stallion and the Secret

Chapter 5

Nightfall's stall was empty.

I panicked, assuming the worst thing that came to my mind.

I forgot to put him in his stall, and now I'll never see him again! He must have trotted off... Who knows where he is? My poor, faithful, horse!

I did the first thing I could think of. I ran out of the stall and to the house as fast as I could run.

"Ryker! Ryker!" I shouted.

I threw the door open, and it almost hit my older brother.

"What is it? What's the matter?" he asked, concern clearly on his face.

"He's—gone! Gone forever and ever!" I despaired.

"*Who?*" Ryker asked, his voice low and his eyes staring right into mine.

"Nightfall!"

"Nightfall?"

I nodded madly. "What am I ever going to do…?"

"Deep breath, Cross Eyes. He mightn't have wandered far. We'll look for him."

I was grateful for my brother's calmness.

For a moment, Ryker silently thought, his eyebrows furrowed in concentration.

We both walked out to the porch.

"Okay," Ryker said, taking the role of leadership. "We'll split up. You can check by the front of the house and down the road to the west. I'll check all over this area and then check the east side of the road. We'll meet right back here after we've searched."

I nodded.

Darting to the front of the house, I looked wildly for the sight of a midnight-black horse.

Nowhere on our land could I see a black stallion. I went to the side of the road and walked briskly down, scanning the area as I did so.

Nightfall wasn't anywhere, and I thought with horror that I might never see him again. I imagined what Dad and Mom would think, and shuddered violently, quickening my pace.

Oh, where is he?

I looked around me, saw no horse, and broke into a run, all the while looking everywhere in my path.

I saw someone—a man—taking a leisurely stroll and darted toward the figure.

"Oh," I panted. "Oh, sir!"

"Why, what ails, lad?" the man asked, giving me a slightly concerned look. He seemed quite dignified and was even wearing a suit.

He gave me a moment to catch my breath.

"Oh, sir!" I exclaimed again. "Please, sir, have you... have you seen... a horse? Big—and solid black..."

The man was perplexed, it appeared. "No, I don't suppose so. Your pony?"

"My stallion—he's... he's gone!" I gasped.

The man nodded. "I see. I'm terribly sorry, but I haven't seen him."

"Thanks anyway," I replied, regaining my breath. "Got to keep searching!"

I darted off again down the side of the road.

I heard the man shout out a "Good luck, lad!"

I ran so much, all the while looking everywhere in front of me and to the sides of me. My heart was pounding like crazy.

While running and looking to the sides, I didn't notice a stone on the ground, and my foot hit it. I lost my balance, yelped, fell, and rolled down into a ditch.

Landing on my back, I began breathing hard, staring up at the sky.

Oh, where is he?

I only stayed lying on my back for a moment—
just to catch my breath—and then I picked myself
up. I got out of the ditch, tried to think clearly as to
what I should do, and pushed my strawberry-blond
bangs out of my eyes.

*If I keep going, I'll get into town soon. Maybe
someone there has seen him.*

I licked my dry lips, then thundered down the
side of the road again.

*He's got to be somewhere—he has to be! It's not
like he could've gone to Hawaii or something; surely
he's somewhere in Wilsonville. He must be!*

A good while went by as I searched with no
avail. I continued stumbling—stumbling on some
rock or branch or nothing at all—but eventually, I
reached the outskirts of the town, darted into an
alley, and found myself at the abandoned bus.

Attempting to catch my breath, I somewhat
hugged the bus, leaning on it with my arms spread
out.

"Oh, bus! Where is he?" I asked, as if the bus
were a living thing that could hear me and
understand me.

I gripped one of the window seals and panted for
breath.

Where is he? Where is he? Where is he? I
thought frantically.

I closed my eyes, put a hand to my thumping
heart, and breathed shakily.

Opening my eyes, I backed away from the bus
and stared at it. The bus was mysterious, seeming to
know secrets it didn't tell. Perhaps I wasn't seeking

hard enough.

Dark clouds were building up in the sky. Far away, lightning appeared.

I was tired, out of breath, and scratched up from my fall in the ditch; I didn't feel like running anymore. I wanted to rest there longer, but Nightfall was still out and about, and I knew not where.

After giving the mystifying bus another look, I darted out of the alley and into the town.

When I got more to the center of Wilsonville, I saw a few people going about their daily lives. I rushed to the nearest person I knew—a nice woman in her late twenties known as Nicole Miller—and asked her if she had seen my horse.

"Oh, Cody, I'm sorry. I haven't."

I thanked her and hurried to another person, and then another.

Wearily, I decided I'd search a little further and dashed off again.

All the while, the sky was looking worse and worse.

How long have I been searching?

I felt languished thinking about how I'd have to go all the way back to the ranch.

I was sweating from all my running, and so when rain started falling, I actually somewhat welcomed it.

When I was somewhat on the outskirts of Wilsonville, I finally gave up, feeling defeated.

I gave myself a moment's rest and then turned back, silently making my way to the ranch, which was a good way away.

I was defeated.

My horse is gone, and it's all my fault. Surely I would've put him in the stable, so I must not have latched the stall.

I stared at my feet as I walked. There was no need to run now, since I was only making my way back to the ranch. The search was over.

I felt miserable and blinked furiously since I didn't want to cry; I was twelve years old, after all!

It's all my fault.

The rain increased, so I picked up my pace some.

Time went slowly. A while later, when I was about halfway through my walk, I broke into a run, for the storm was getting worse.

The same mistake was almost made twice because I stumbled on the same stone that had caused me to fall into the ditch earlier that day. This time, however, I kept myself from falling and afterward reminded myself to be a little more careful. After all, it was raining; the ground was slippery.

Lost in my own miserable thoughts, I felt very gloomy.

However, I was jolted out of my despair when I heard something.

I stopped in my tracks and held my breath. I closed my eyes, listening to the sound.

Thud, thud, thud...

My eyes flew open, and I gasped.

Before me, a midnight-colored stallion galloped out of the bushes, and with shock I realized that the rider on it was my uncle.

* * *

"Nightfall!" I exclaimed.

Uncle Colton made Nightfall halt. Wrapping my arms around my horse's neck, I was very much relieved.

"Oh, Nightfall," I breathed.

I stopped hugging my horse and looked up at my uncle.

"I've been looking everywhere!" I said. "He's my horse, though. You should've—"

"—asked?" Uncle Colton finished for me.

I nodded.

Uncle Colton shrugged. "Well, sorry. Didn't think you'd mind. Actually, I was doing you a favor. Exercised your horse for you and all."

Observing my horse, I realized he had given Nightfall a workout, all right.

"Wait, he's *overworked!*" I declared. "He needs to rest. You must have ridden him for a long time. I've been searching so long… Ryker too."

Mentioning my brother made me recall something.

I yelled, "I'll be right back," and then I dashed to the ranch.

I checked the patio, then inside the house, calling out for my brother. After this, I checked the buildings outside, hollering.

Ryker was clearly still searching faithfully— more than he needed to.

I darted back to Uncle Colton.

"Ryker must still be searching for Nightfall! I've *got* to go look for him. Could you take care of Nightfall and let him rest? I'll take one of the other horses—Trigger, I suppose—and look for him."

I didn't wait for a response. I rushed back to the stable, saddled up Trigger, got on, and hurried off, one hand pushing my hat down more firmly and the other hand grasping the reins.

I scanned the road constantly, ignoring the rain. I was so relieved to not be running anymore, instead letting Trigger take care of it.

Trigger is Ryker's horse—his trusty, we say. Ryker takes very good care of him, and they have won lots of rodeo competitions together. Trigger had seemed like the natural choice to bring along, since he's Pitchfork's. (He is fine with me riding him, and one of the reasons why is probably because I bring him carrots sometimes. Ryker's his favorite, though, of course.)

Lightning thundered overhead, and I leaned forward a little.

Poor Ryker! I thought. *Out in the rain…*

"Ryker!" I yelled out into the distance. "Where are you? Nightfall's been found! Where are you, Ryker?"

I shouted this out for quite a while and was getting tired of it, since no one was hearing it anyway, but I sighed in relief when I saw a figure a little way off, seemingly staring up at the sky.

"Oh, Ryker!" I exclaimed. "Is it you?"

The figure heard me shout and turned around. I could clearly see who it was. He came running.

"Cody! Did you find Nightfall?"

I brought Trigger to a stop and slipped off him.

Quickly, I told Ryker what had happened—that

Uncle Colton had taken Nightfall riding.

"He should have asked you first!" Ryker replied.

Both of us got up on the trusty stallion.

"I know," I said, "but he was riding him to give him exercise. I suppose it's all right."

"He overworked him, though! That's irresponsible."

"I-I know…"

"He should've said something—made a note."

"Yes, that would have been a good idea…" I said softly.

I was silent for a moment, relieved but concerned for my horse's wellbeing.

"Thanks for helping me search."

"No problem, but you're kind of scratched up. What happened?"

"Oh, I fell into a ditch," I replied casually.

"*What?*"

"I tripped on a stone."

"I guess I shouldn't be surprised; you're Cody."

Shivering in the rain, I at least had my brother's comment to laugh at.

* * *

"Oh, I'm glad!" exclaimed Fay in earnest.

"As am I," said Lydia from inside the bus. "What an unfortunate time for the rain to come."

I nodded in agreement but added, "I imagine the wheat field was glad for the moisture."

Fay, Lia, and I were at the bus the next day, after school. I was filling them in about the previous evening's events.

As stated earlier, Lia was inside the bus. She was

searching around for some book to help us with history. Fay was sitting on the bus steps, making a list of things we needed to memorize. I, however, was sitting on the bus roof—something the girls always found amusing.

The bus is stuffed with books—so stuffed that it isn't easy for us all to fit in. It's possible but claustrophobic—that is, crowded. There was a time when the three of us, plus Ryker, were all in the bus, and after that experience I'm pretty sure Pitchfork could be diagnosed with claustrophobia.

"It's got to be here somewhere…" Lia said. "But where did I put it? I think maybe I'd forget my head if it weren't attached…"

"No, that would be Cody," Fay teasingly replied.

I could hear Lydia laugh a little at Fay's statement, but then she was quiet, searching in concentration.

It was to Felicia's and my surprise when Lia came out of the bus holding what seemed most certainly to be a newspaper in her hands.

When she walked onto the bus steps, my dangling feet accidently hit her in the forehead. I guess sitting right above the school bus door wasn't a wise idea. Good thing I wasn't wearing spurs, at least!

Concentrating on the paper, though, she didn't say anything about my feet hitting her head.

Fay had gotten up from where she had been sitting on the steps so that Lia could get back to the ground, but when she stood up…

"Ack, Cody! Get your feet out of the way!"

"Sorry!"

"Hey, guys!" Lydia said. "Get a load of this newspaper I found. The year says 1995 and the date is the seventeenth of August."

Lydia and Fay were scanning the paper.

"So, I just turned four," I replied, laughing a little and climbing down the bus.

"Look at the advertisements," Felicia chirped with interest.

I was just about to take a good look at the paper myself, when Lydia took a step backwards, had a surprised look on her face, and put a hand to her mouth.

"Why, what's the matter, Lia?" Fay asked, her blue eyes wide with concern.

Lydia folded up the newspaper quickly, and when I came up to her, she took another step back.

"What's up?" I asked, confused.

"Just a second," she replied, and then went a little way away from me. She opened the paper up again and called for Fay to come look at whatever it was that had her acting so unusual.

She showed Fay, who scanned the paper and then also looked distressed.

"Hey, what is it?" I asked, getting a little impatient.

Both girls were silent.

"What is it?" I repeated more loudly.

Fay was at a loss for words, it seemed.

For a while, Lia was the same. Eventually, she went over to me, fumbled with the paper a little, found whatever dreadful thing was typed out on it, and showed me, saying, "Cody, um… I… I don't think you're going to like this."

I'm certain my face turned just as upset as Lia and Fay's had upon seeing the text.

Sixth Grade's End

Chapter 6

"No!" I somewhat yelled.

I was disappointed—disappointed in Fay and Lydia.

It was impossible to read the expression on Lia's face, but Felicia appeared distressed.

I didn't believe the report, and neither girl said a thing.

Upset, I declared, "It isn't true!"

"Cody—"

"It isn't!" I snapped, cutting Lia off.

Fay quietly grabbed the paper from my hands and scanned over it again. She was silent, contemplating.

Lydia tried to speak again, and I let her.

"This i-isn't the first time… the first time something happened like that…"

"Like what?" I asked, feeling cross and not making the connection.

Lia's cheeks turned slightly pink, and she looked at the ground, avoiding my gaze.

"Betrayal," she gasped out softly.

Her point clicked with me, but I doubt it had the intended effect.

"That's like apples to oranges!" I burst out.

Fay looked up from the newspaper and stared at me with a surprised and shocked look.

"Kodiak!" she burst out.

I realized my comment came out cruelly. After all, the three of us had encountered a horrible betrayal just earlier that year which clearly would've hit Lydia the hardest.

A rift seemed to spread between me and Lia.

"I guess you're right, to an extent," Lydia said flatly yet softly. "For me, it was taken to a whole different level. *I'm* an orphan."

Then, quietly, hurt—though not furious—she turned around and walked off. It was anything but an angry storming off. It was much calmer, as if she was trying to keep the rift from growing by temporarily remaining silent.

I was staring at where Lia had been, and Fay was staring at me.

"You should apologize," she said simply. Then she gushed out, "Oh, Cody, I'm terribly sorry about the paper. I understand it's very aggravating and shocking and just must feel horrible! But please…"

I nodded, feeling less annoyed than I had been feeling.

"I... I'm sorry," I said. "And, I'll apologize to her—right now. But, I just don't—I can't—believe that newspaper is true."

Fay didn't say anything. She still seemed to be thinking to herself. She didn't want to believe what she read, and I realized that neither had Lia.

"I'll be back," I told Fay and then went to find my other friend.

She wasn't far; I found her deep in thought, leaning up against a nearby building.

"Lia!" I shouted to get her attention.

She turned to look at me and was about to speak, but I did so instead.

"I... I shouldn't have—shouldn't have acted the way I did." Still feeling embarrassed, I added, "I... I was rude."

My apology made, I felt heat rise to my cheeks.

Lydia surprised me, however, with an apology of her own.

"Oh, but Cody! I should have used more tact—been more sensitive. You needed time to think about what you just read. Surely *I'm* to blame as well."

The horrible memory of what I had read in that newspaper came back.

It cannot be true.

* * *

Tomorrow is the last day of school, I thought with a feeling of excitement yet also with a sense of disappointment.

I was walking up the staircase, headed to my

bedroom.

After this, sixth grade will be over forever, and I'll be off to Beaver City for seventh grade.

Most likely, Fay was at her house feeling depressed. She loved school—loved learning new things every day. She'd have to endure a whole summer without her beloved classes.

I was going to miss the school building. It was filled with many memories. And I'll admit, not all of them were pleasant, but I had grown fond of the place. Just… not quite like Fay had.

Lia liked school, but she also liked summer vacation. The memories of school were probably more powerful for her, though, than for me.

I stopped walking up the staircase and stood halfway up.

I've always wondered how she's able to walk through that school every day—see those rooms, see the memories of the past…

There had to be many painful memories for her now, so much that I got to thinking.

"What are you doing just standing on the staircase, Cross Eyes?"

I snapped out of my thoughts and turned to Ryker.

"Hey, Pitchfork," I replied. "Guess I just got to thinking."

"Well that's new," my brother teased. "You? Thinking?"

I playfully rolled my eyes.

"I think a lot. Trust me."

"Anyway, what are you thinking about?"

"Well, the last day of school's tomorrow…"

"Yeah. You'll be at my school, though," Ryker said, grinning.

I nodded. "I've got mixed feelings, though; I like this school. And then I got to thinking about how it must be hard for Lia to go to this school every day…"

Ryker understood what I meant; he knew exactly what kind of stuff I had been referring to.

"I've wondered that also. It must feel pretty awful at times."

"Yeah…" I agreed quietly. "But somehow she does it—and acts normal, too."

"She's unique," Ryker stated with a little smile.

I was about to reply, but then Ryker let out a little laugh, saying, "Look at us! Now we're *both* standing on the staircase."

I realized my brother was right, and we both hurried up the stairs. He turned one direction and I turned the other, but then I abruptly stopped.

I stared at the sight in front of me.

To myself, I whispered, "The door…"

Dad and Mom's bedroom door was opened a crack.

"Again?" I breathed and pushed the door open.

The pendulum was swinging. I surveyed the bedroom.

"What's going on…?" I wondered aloud. "Why'd this happen *twice?*"

I looked under the bed. Nothing, of course.

For a split second, I recalled what that newspaper had said and shuddered.

I looked around more.

"Strange…" I mumbled. "So strange. Not a thing seems out of place."

My original intent for even going upstairs was to go to my bedroom and work on that hot pad I had been knitting. Now, however, I went out of my parents' room, shut the door, and walked *down* the stairs, trying to make sense of the situation.

"I ought to check Father's office," I said to myself.

I did just that, walking across the house to my destination.

However, upon approaching the office door, I heard noise. It was coming from inside the office.

I sucked in my breath and darted behind Mom's display cabinet.

A burglar broke into the house—I just know it!

For a while, I remained where I was, feeling worried. Then, it occurred to me that it would be very unlikely for a thief to have come into the house; after all, it was broad daylight! I actually grinned a little, finding my suspicion humorous.

However, the smile faded away quickly when the door to the office opened and I saw a man silently slip out.

My heart jumped.

No… No, no, no!

Before my eyes, I saw a man with several papers in his hands, leaving.

The hallway I was in was dimly lit, but a horrifying dread swept over me at the sight. For when I saw the man leave, I yet again recalled what I had read on that newspaper. Silently pulling it out of my pocket—I had taken the paper with me from the bus—I read under my breath:

> *In hot water yesterday, Colton Honeysett, a bull rider who has participated in countless rodeos in Wyoming, was found guilty of using illegally sharpened spurs. Competition rules limit which spur types and lengths are permitted. Honeysett's spurs would increase the height of bulls' kicks by an unfair proportion, resulting in higher scores. He has been fined and disqualified from his latest rodeo.*

My heart sank like a stone.

* * *

It isn't true... It isn't true. It's fake!

I was in my bedroom, knitting away at the hot pad.

I breathed deeply.

"It's *so* untrue that I won't even *waste* my time thinking about it," I told myself firmly. "Besides, even if it were true, it'd clearly be an accident. Uncle Colton wouldn't cheat in a rodeo. I've seen him myself; he's too good at riding horses to ever have a reason for wanting to cheat."

I contemplated that for a while and felt convinced.

My mind at rest, I enjoyed the fresh air coming

in through the opened window as well as the sunshine and chirping birds. I felt much more at ease.

I'll invite the girls to come over tomorrow. Besides, it's a tradition for them to come to my house on the last day of school—no need to break the custom.

I was happy now.

"And, it'll help jerk Fay out of her school-is-over depression," I said aloud.

It occurred to me that I should make more snickerdoodles. The girls and I always had snickerdoodles for the last day of school. Then again, when *don't* we have them?

For a moment, my hands stilled from my knitting, and I stared out the window, gazing at the wheat field. It looked beautiful—beautiful, indeed.

Looking down at my knitted work, a small grin spread over my face—the hot pad was complete.

Mom will love it, I thought.

A moment of longing filled me. I hadn't heard from either of my parents in about a week—which was absurd—and I didn't know how I was supposed to contact them. There wasn't an address that I could mail a letter to, and when I tried calling my father's phone, there was no response. Anyway, I had been pushing these concerns away for some time. However, the feeling which reminded me of a tugging on the sleeve had come back now. It occurred to me, though, that my parents should be returning the day after tomorrow, at latest. They had said they might be gone seventeen days, as opposed to fourteen. Well, today was the fifteenth day.

Oh, they're fine! I told myself. *Perhaps Dad's phone just got broken—fell in the water or something.*

"No need to assume the worst," I said aloud, rolling the hot pad up and tying a pale-pink ribbon around the whole thing. "They'll be back soon."

* * *

It was the last day of sixth grade.

The morning routine was, for the most part, the same. However, I had slept through my alarm, but Ryker came to my rescue, waking me up in time. Later, I thundered down the stairs holding all the things I needed to take to school. While storming down, I almost fell due to my arms being so full. Once I got off the staircase, I dropped everything down by the front door.

Then, I headed to the kitchen, where I made my infamous pancakes.

I also made my own syrup... sort of. It wasn't maple syrup at all, but it was really good. A good time earlier, I got the idea for the recipe. It consists of cream, honey, and a little cinnamon, all mixed up. Now, don't get me wrong; maple syrup is good, but I felt we needed something a little extra special today.

Ryker entered the kitchen after a little while, having done some of his chores. He yawned and poured himself a cup of coffee. I grinned to myself upon remembering how Fay and Lia had too much caffeine when they had a sleepover. It was a funny memory, and I let out a small snort.

"Good morning, Pitchfork," I chirped.

"Thanks. You too, Cross Eyes."

"Where's Uncle Colton?" I asked, sticking my tongue out in concentration as I poured some batter on the griddle. I was trying to make an ultra-huge pancake!

"Oh, I don't know," Ryker said, heaving a sigh. He was one of those people who could drink coffee black, without anything in it, and like it. Not me, though. If Mom lets me have coffee—and she does, occasionally—it's going to have loads of coconut sugar and cream. Only a little coffee with my sweetener, please.

I disregarded Uncle Colton's absence. "The girls are coming over this afternoon, by the way."

"Did you invite them?"

"Yeah, called them last night."

"And you didn't let me know until now?" Ryker asked with a slight laugh.

"It's the last day of school," I replied, "and we *always* hang out on the last day of school."

"Don't forget the snickerdoodles," Ryker added.

I nodded in agreement. "Yes, certainly. What would the last day of school be like without such?"

"Horrid."

I laughed at my brother's response.

"Of course."

* * *

"It's the end of sixth grade—the beginning of summer vacation. Fay's going to be hysterical," said Lydia.

Lia and I were walking down the sidewalk to Fay's house. School was starting in an hour, so we weren't too rushed and decided that instead of riding our bicycles, we would just walk.

"No doubt she'll lose it," I said in agreement with my brunette friend.

"First today, then summer, then off to Beaver City for all of us!" Lia chirped. "But, honestly, I like the school here. It's too bad we can't stay longer."

"I know, right?"

"So many memories," said Lydia. "I guess we'll just have to make more memories at the new school!"

After chatting a little more, we both fell silent. I felt a little awkward, recalling the newspaper we had read just the day before. There was no way Lia forgot about it, but she didn't say anything on the matter. I was okay with that.

"Well, here's Fay's," Lia said softly, breaking the silence. She pointed to the two-story house that came into view.

Fay's house was Victorian in style, with vines climbing up the white walls outside. The shingles were gray, and there was a cone-shaped roof on part of the house, kind of like a castle. It was the roof of Fay's room. Her house is very cool and has existed for a very long time.

We opened the black, metal gate; walked up the decorative, curvy concrete which led us to her front porch; and then walked up the porch steps. I rang the doorbell and could hear the pretty chime sound.

A moment passed, and then Mrs. Blackwood opened the door.

"Oh, hello, children. Won't you come in?"

Lia and I stepped in and were greeted by Fay's little, white dog, Gracie. Gracie was wearing a pink tutu, which was usually the case and no surprise. Such a thing was Felicia's idea, and rarely was Gracie seen otherwise.

"Where's Fay?" I asked Mrs. Blackwood.

Mrs. Blackwood laughed a little. "She's up in her room. She was saying something about trying to find her blue hairbow."

I snickered. "Really? I should think she'd be looking for a *pink* one."

"Well, she's already wearing a pink dress," Mrs. Blackwood replied, "so, I guess she doesn't want to overdo it. Also, she said the blue bow matched the jeans she's wearing."

"I didn't know she believed overdoing pink was possible."

Lia laughed a little.

There are two things about Fay that pretty much anyone can see: She loves the color pink, and she loves dresses. However, Fay is not vain; she's actually quite frugal, and even makes a lot of her own clothing—which I think is super cool.

Grinning, Lydia said, "Maybe I can help her find her bow." She then excused herself, heading up the stairs.

"Anyway, how's Leanne?" I asked Mrs. Blackwood. "Are you emotional that she's started walking now?"

Mrs. Blackwood nodded. "Yes, I am. Reece was making fun of me because I was shedding some tears when she took her first steps last week."

Reece is the name of Fay's father.

"Really?" I asked. "I don't see him tease people much."

Mrs. Blackwood smiled. "Well, he does occasionally tease, though not very often."

I chatted with Fay's mother a little longer and then headed up the stairs to see the girls.

I just made my way to the top of the stairs when I heard Lia shout, "Found it!"

Fay's door was wide open, and her room was... Well, they had certainly been searching for the bow. Hair accessories were all over Fay's bed!

"Well, well, well," I said with a smirk. "I'm impressed, Fay. I don't think I've *ever* seen your room this messy in my entire twelve—going on thirteen—years of living."

Fay turned to me and playfully waved her hand as if shooing away a pesky fly.

"Desperate times call for desperate measures," she stated.

"And for Fay," Lia began, "a missing hairbow counts as such."

The girls set all the hair accessories in a basket and then put it away so that Fay's room was once again its tidy self.

"You wouldn't understand, Kodiak," said Fay, carefully putting the hairbow in her sandy-brown curls, which were in a high ponytail. "After all, you're a boy."

"It'd be the equivalent of you losing a snickerdoodle," Lia explained.

"Okay, well that puts a whole new perspective on

the matter."

"Oh, but Lia," Fay began, changing the subject somewhat, "I love your whale hairclip."

Lydia loves sea creatures—especially whales. Her father used to be the manager of three aquariums. We went to one of them—the one in Ashland—a couple of months ago on the first day of spring.

"Thanks!" Lia replied. "Grandmother gave it to me as an early birthday present."

Lydia was turning thirteen soon—on the twelfth of June.

I half-listened to the rest of their conversation, zoning out into my own thoughts. After all, they were just talking about girly things like hair accessories and dresses and pink.

"Anyway," Fay began after a while, "I guess we better be going. We don't want to be late."

I looked at Fay's pink alarm clock and realized she was right; we needed to leave.

Lia and I thumped down the stairs, getting to the end of the spiraling staircase first, and then Fay, who hadn't "thumped" down, arrived at the end about ten seconds later.

Fay's mom had already left. She needed to leave early so that she could get to Lydia's house on time. Lia's grandmother was going to babysit Leanne since Mrs. Blackwood would be teaching at school today.

In a moment, the three of us were heading out of the house. Fay locked the door, and then we walked down the porch steps onto the curvy concrete, exiting through the black, metal gate.

* * *

The school day was good. I paid attention reasonably well in my classes so that Lia only had to kick me in the shin twice. Also, I totally *aced* the fifty-yard dash we did, which was awesome! Currently, there were only minutes left in the school day; I knew the bell would ring soon and that all the sixth graders would gather up their stuff and leave that building for good. It was a strange feeling, knowing I wouldn't be there when the new school year started.

"I'm glad I got to teach each of you," Mrs. Blackwood said. "I wish you much luck with the new school year. Remember to study and do *all* your homework."

She looked at me teasingly when she said that last sentence, and I grinned a little. Some of the other kids noticed this and giggled.

Then the bell rang. All the students scurried out of their chairs, gathered up their stuff, and filed out of the classroom faster than a pack of wild hyenas.

Well, that's that. It's all over, finished forever.

I was just about to exit the classroom when suddenly, I hesitated by the doorway. Other than Felica and Lydia, all the other kids had already left class.

"Go ahead, girls. I'll catch up in a minute," I told them.

Fay tilted her head a little, but Lia nodded. They both thanked Mrs. Blackwood for teaching them and then left—after Fay gave her mother a hug, of

78

course.

I walked over to Mrs. Blackwood and faintly grinned at her.

"Can I help you with something, Kodiak?" Mrs. Blackwood asked kindly.

I shrugged and looked at the ground, thinking about what I was going to say.

"Just... wanting to say thanks for teaching," I told Mrs. Blackwood. I turned my head up and looked her straight in the eyes. She had the same eye color as Fay's—light blue. "I think I've learned more than I expected to since you started teaching temporarily for these few months."

Mrs. Blackwood smiled. "I'm glad to hear it. Do you have any ideas on what you want to do for a career one day?"

"Well... I like farming—like my Dad and Uncle Colton! But... I also like astronomy."

Mrs. Blackwood nodded. "I wish you good luck on whichever one you decide to pursue one day."

"Thanks. You're a *really* good teacher, though. I bet you're one of the reasons why Fay's so smart! It'd be really cool if you'd teach at Beaver City next year, but I know you want to be a housewife and stay home with Leanne. Still... maybe you should consider being, like... a substitute teacher...?"

She looked a little surprised. "Well, I... I don't know. Though I'm glad you've enjoyed having me teach you."

"Would you consider it?"

"I suppose so. Thank you, Kodiak."

I beamed.

"No, thank *you.*"

I looked at the doorway.

"I guess I should get going, though. Thanks again for teaching, Mrs. Blackwood. Bye!"

"Goodbye, Cody. Don't forget to read over the summer!"

"Okay, '*Mom,*'" I teasingly replied with a laugh, lightheartedly rolling my eyes.

I exited that classroom feeling happy, but then I felt gradually sadder as I got further away. I realized, however, that it was time to accept reality.

Letting go is part of living.

* * *

"I guess this is it," I said to the girls, one hand on the school's outside wall. "One more minute here at the school and then off to my house for snickerdoodles."

"Yup," Lia said, staring at the building. "I'll miss this place."

"Me too..." Fay agreed. She looked gloomy. "I'm going to do extra studying over the summer, though; there's so much to learn."

"Oh, Fay," I said fondly, "you're always so devoted to knowledge."

"It's a good way to be," Lydia agreed. "I like school, but I just don't feel like sitting down and staring at a history book all summer."

"But when you're studying history, you get to— oh, look!" Fay exclaimed. Then she lowered her voice. "Trevin's coming toward us..."

Trevin Aragon came up, a faint smirk on his face.

"Hello," he directly said to me.

"Hi…" I replied.

Lia and Fay eyed Trevin, but he didn't pay much attention to them.

"What's your uncle like?" Trevin asked.

"I like him very much," I replied, cautiously eyeing the bully. "Uncle Colton's a *real* cowboy."

Trevin held his head up high.

"Hmm."

The memory of the newspaper crossed my mind. *Maybe he's heard about that… It isn't true!*

Trevin looked me in the eyes and leaned in a little.

"You know he cheated, don't you?" he whispered.

Fay and Lia heard Trevin.

I felt my cheeks getting pink.

"No he didn't!" I burst out. "Uncle Colton wouldn't!"

"Or would he?" Trevin asked with a sneer.

Fay's temper was rising quickly.

"Stop!" she said sharply. "What are you trying to prove?"

Trevin looked at Fay and smirked a little.

"That he isn't who you think he is."

Fay narrowed her ice-blue eyes.

I inhaled harshly.

Trevin looked back at me.

"Colton Honeysett cheated!" he burst out.

I noticed a couple of other kids heard Trevin and edged a little closer.

"Trevin!" Fay shouted. "You're *cruel.*"

"Am I, Felicia?" he asked. "Am I really, now? I always thought that *cheating* was cruel. Unlike Cody, I'm all A's, and unlike his family, I earn my success. I *never* cheat—not one bit!"

Lydia, who had remained quiet until now, replied softly, "And since when was coming and telling someone unsympathetically that their uncle is a cheater—even if it is true—not cruel?"

Trevin couldn't give a good response to that, so he started chanting, "Cheater! Cheater!"

A few other kids started chanting it too, though they probably didn't know who Trevin was talking about.

"Cheater! Cheater!"

The chant was getting others' attention, and the number of chanting schoolkids was growing.

Stop it, stop it, stop it... I pleaded in my head.

They didn't stop. The number of chanting kids only grew. Even some little kids—kindergartners and first graders and second graders—who barely knew me if they knew me at all, joined in. But they were caught up in the chant and wanted to join in with the bigger kids. It was savagery.

Fay wasn't going to have it for another minute.

"Stop it, I say!" she exclaimed. "Stop it!"

Lydia wasn't pleased either.

"You don't even know why you're chanting!" she yelled over the ruckus. "You don't even..."

Most of the others didn't care, though; they went on chanting anyway.

Fay and Lia continued trying to get the kids to stop, but it was no use.

"Come on, girls," I said, "let's just go."

We did just that, and I deeply hoped the kids at school wouldn't follow us. To my immense relief, they didn't. Most of them I'd never see again.

Once we got out of sight, we broke into a run and stayed running all the way until we reached my property.

Panting for breath, I said, "That didn't go so well."

Felicia nodded furiously.

Lia looked a little glum.

"That was absurd," she said. "They didn't even know what was going on."

"We couldn't even... couldn't even leave the school in peace—on our last day!" I said in annoyance.

Fay was quiet; I knew she must have been deep in thought.

"Those others..." she said after a little while of quiet. "They... How could they be so... so..."

"Rude? Cruel?" I inquired. I was indignant. "I don't know."

No one spoke for a while.

Suddenly, Lia just started heading for the house.

Halfway to the house, Lydia turned around.

"Well? Aren't you coming? Surely we aren't going to let *them* spoil our fun now, are we? This is the start of summer vacation!"

I realized Lydia had a point. We could either choose to be gloomy, or we could choose to go have fun.

Fay smiled a little. "You're right, Lia."

"Okay, then," I said, my spirits beginning to rise. "I'm with you girls. Let's go have some snickerdoodles."

As I walked to the house, a little thought nagged in my mind.

Under my breath, I whispered, "Now I've just *got* to prove Uncle Colton's innocence."

Fun and Games

Chapter 7

"Dunk it!" Lia shouted.

The girls and I were outside, shooting baskets.

Running to the basketball goal and then jumping up, I slammed the ball into the goal. I beamed.

I then threw the ball to Lydia.

"Now you do it," I told her, smirking.

"I guess I could try," she replied, catching the ball. "After all, the goal isn't raised all the way up…"

She started a good distance away and took off running. When she jumped up, however, she couldn't go high enough. She did get close, though.

"I can't do it," Lydia said with a laugh. "You try,

Fay."

"Oh no," Felicia murmured. "I'm not even good at shooting the ball, let alone dunking it."

Lia and I cheered Fay on.

"Do it! Do it! Do it!"

Fay gave in.

"Okay, fine. But don't expect me to be able to jump high enough."

Fay never was much into athletics, and shooting hoops certainly hadn't been her idea.

Like Lia and I did, Fay took off running and jumped up, but she didn't even come close to dunking it.

She sighed and said, "What did I tell you guys?"

"How about you let *me* show you how it's done."

We all turned to where the voice came from and saw Ryker—holding a snickerdoodle. He had apparently just come from the kitchen.

"Okay," Fay said, "show us what you got."

Ryker quickly finished his snickerdoodle, like any sensible person would do, and took the basketball.

He showed off a little with the ball, then ran a few feet, leaped up in the air higher than I had, slammed the ball into the net, and landed on his feet with a thump.

The girls and I applauded him.

"That was awesome!" I chirped. "Did you learn to jump that high with Micah?"

Micah was one of Ryker's friends from high school. He lived in Beaver City. I didn't know him extremely well, but I knew that he and Ryker liked to shoot hoops together.

"Well, I certainly got a lot of practice from him," Ryker responded.

"We should see if Uncle Colton wants to play soon," I said.

"Where is he, anyway?" Ryker asked. "I haven't seen him since this morning, before we left for school."

I shrugged. "I don't know. I imagine he'll show up eventually. After all, he's got to meet the girls!"

Lydia and Felicia were bouncing the ball back and forth to each other as Ryker and I talked.

"Maybe he went to… shop for groceries?" Fay asked.

"Probably not," I replied, "since we don't really need any at the moment."

Lydia was silent, thinking.

"Maybe he's visiting your parents' friends," she said, shooting a basket.

"Maybe," Ryker replied. "Where's Uriah?"

"In the house," I said. "Maybe he'll play basketball with us?"

Ryker didn't answer that question but instead said, "I was hoping Dad and Mom would be back yesterday."

Fay tilted her head and looked at me. "When are they supposed to come back?"

"Definitely by tomorrow," I answered, catching the ball as Lia threw it to me.

"Have you heard from them?" Lydia inquired.

"No," I replied, landing a bank shot, "not since a week ago."

I threw the ball at Ryker, who caught it with ease and then said, "And it's unusual for them not to call—especially Mom."

Felicia furrowed her brow.

"Why don't *you* just call *them?*" she asked in an obvious manner.

Ryker sighed.

"I tried that already—twice every day—after we didn't hear from them in a while," he explained. "No one answered."

"Hmm…" Lydia muttered. "That's strange—and concerning."

It was at this moment when I noticed Uriah getting into his pickup.

"Hey, Uriah!" I shouted. "Want to shoot baskets with us?"

Uriah is *really* good at basketball. He plays it with us on weekends.

He didn't reply, though. Instead, he started his truck and drove off, not even paying attention to any of us.

"Hmm," I said. "Perhaps he didn't hear me—and I really wanted to play basketball with him, too! He can land all *kinds* of cool-looking shots."

"I have to agree with that," Ryker replied.

"Well," Lia began, "maybe he'll join us later."

"In the meantime," I said with a smirk, "I'm going to get myself a snickerdoodle—or six."

* * *

We had been playing basketball for another half an hour when Uncle Colton's muddy truck drove up. My spirits rose.

"Girls!" I exclaimed. "Now you can *finally* meet my uncle."

"Okay," Lydia said, setting our basketball down. "Do you think he'll play this with us?"

"Hopefully," I replied.

Uncle Colton parked, shut off the truck, and began walking toward the house—which was toward us.

"Hi, Uncle Colton!" I chirped. "These are my friends. This one's Felicia Blackwood—or, of course, Fay—and this is Lydia Arlington, also known as Lia."

Fay waved with a smile, and Lydia politely held out a hand to shake.

Both of the girls had decided that even if what the newspaper said *was* true—which I certainly didn't believe could be a possibility—Uncle Colton could have changed his ways since then. They would give him a chance.

"How are you, sir?" Lia asked.

"Fine, thanks," Uncle Colton replied and smiled.

Fay felt a little awkward, it seemed.

"Cody's said a lot about you," she said shyly.

"Yeah. Said a lot about you too, so I guess it's about time we met."

I laughed, and Lia smiled a little.

"It's nice to meet someone Cody's so fond of."

"I'll never remember your names, though," my uncle replied. "Never been any good at that."

Ryker raised an eyebrow.

"It's just Lydia and Felicia; how hard is it to remember that? Or, you could always say Lia and

Fay."

"I guess so. Anyway, sorry to break up the conversation, but I'm going to the horses, now. Nice to meet ya—Lydia and, um... Felicia, right?"

And with that, Uncle Colton walked off to the stables.

"Well…" Fay said, slightly uncertain, "he seems nice enough."

"I knew you'd like him," I chirped, looking at where my uncle left. "He's great!"

* * *

A while later, the girls and I were going to play hide-and-seek. Fay was the seeker, and I was hiding in a stable. As for Lia, she had darted for the wheat field.

I had been hiding for a little while now, and while I was hiding, Ryker came in. Uncle Colton was already in here.

From what I could see, Ryker's facial expression turned from a neutral look, to a surprised one, and then to displeasure.

"Uncle Colton!" Ryker gasped. "I said you shouldn't ride Blizzard!"

"He needed exercise."

"Father instructed me to take care of him," Pitchfork explained. "He didn't want even *Cody* to ride him—and that horse *likes* Cody."

"Well, I'm Nolan's brother-in-law, so I'm sure he doesn't mind."

"But he *said*... He *said* that he only wanted me to ride him! I wouldn't have an issue with you riding him if Dad had said that it was okay, but he didn't, and I've been riding Blizzard every day after school."

"Why didn't you today?"

"I was going to! It's just that before I did, Cody asked me to shoot baskets and stuff first."

In the corner of the stable, I hid myself by sneaking into some straw.

Don't mind me, I thought. *Just hiding from Fay.*

They went back and forth about Blizzard for a while longer when I saw Fay slip in through the door. She looked uneasy—which is no surprise, considering she stepped in while there was an argument going on.

"Well," Uncle Colton began, "it turned out fine anyway, so I don't see the point in this conversation."

"You didn't have the authority to ride him to begin with!" Ryker retorted. "That's the point."

"Oh, stop trying to be so perfect all the time!" Uncle Colton shouted, indignant. "I'm sick of you."

My heart leaped at the words, and I saw from my hiding spot that Fay put a hand to her mouth and gasped.

Ryker was stunned speechless at Uncle Colton's statement. He quickly turned around upon hearing Felicia.

"Fay?" he asked. "Why are you in here?"

Fay blushed. "I-I was—we're playing hide-and-seek, and I'm looking for the others… I wasn't trying to eavesdrop."

Pitchfork gave one nod and then turned back to Uncle Colton. My brother didn't say a word but stared at the man with whom he shared so much similarity in appearance.

Uncle Colton stormed out of the stable.

I stood out of my hiding place, brushing the straw off myself, and Fay saw me but didn't speak.

I stared at my older brother. "Pitchfork?"

"Oh. What is it?"

"I-I heard… Surely he… He didn't… He didn't mean it."

Ryker's blue eyes were fiery with hurt and indignation.

"No, Cody. He *did* mean it. He's sick of me."

"But, Pitchfork…"

"No. He doesn't listen."

"He couldn't have truly meant that; you're his nephew."

"Who said blood's thicker than water?"

Fay, preferring to let us converse in private, said, "Please excuse me."

And with that, she slipped out of the barn, likely going to find Lydia, who must have still been hiding.

"But Ryker…" was all I could say.

"It's… It isn't good, Cross Eyes. Why don't Dad and Mom answer? I'm worried—for them, for us."

I felt uneasy.

"They've got to be fine," I said.

Though, I couldn't think of any evidence for that.

"And if they aren't? What then? I'm sixteen and you're twelve."

I decided to hold off on explaining how I was going on thirteen.

"They could still arrive tomorrow, Ryker."

"Yes, Cody, but I'm beginning to lose hope."

I stared at my brother.

"Maybe they just haven't thought to call."

"They wouldn't forget," Ryker declared. "Not ever."

"Maybe Dad dropped his phone down into a lake and it got destroyed."

That was the best idea I could come up with, though it sounded really lame.

"I mean, I guess it's possible, but I just don't know—doesn't seem all that likely."

I gave a solemn nod.

"Yes, Pitchfork, but… it's almost all the hope we've got."

* * *

The next day passed, and my parents did not return. A week later, they *still* weren't back.

"Something must have happened," Ryker said, concern clearly in his voice. "There's no explanation other than that."

Deep down, I felt he must be right, though I wouldn't let myself accept it.

"Maybe Uncle Colton could help us…" I said.

"No," Ryker replied stiffly. "I'm sure he knows as much as we do. We need help."

"Should we contact Mr. and Mrs. Blackwood?" I asked.

"Perhaps."

My brother and I walked outside, and my gaze landed on the wheat field. Its golden glory gave me a sense of home—of family. Only… the family wasn't quite complete like it was before.

"Maybe the authorities? The police?" Ryker said aloud, though more to himself than anyone else.

My heart fluttered. Such a statement seemed to imply things I couldn't bring myself to say.

"Uncle Colton will know what to do," I said.

Ryker gave me a look I couldn't quite place.

"I don't know, Cross Eyes."

I thought for a moment.

"Well…" I began, "Uncle Colton is Mother's brother… I'm sure he'll contact the police for us."

Pitchfork sighed.

"Perhaps… I guess. You… You ask him. He'd listen to you."

My older brother turned away from me, and I saw his fists clench.

I nodded a little, though Ryker couldn't see me.

"I'll tell him right now," I said.

"Thanks…"

Running into the house, I knocked urgently on Uncle Colton's door and shouted for him.

It took a moment until he opened up the door, and when he did, he eyed me in curiosity.

"What?" he told me.

"I think we should call the police!"

"Because?"

"Mom and Dad were supposed to come back at latest a *week* ago!"

"So? Maybe they got busy—met old friends and chatted a while."

"But they haven't called on the phone or anything."

"Ya scared?"

I blushed.

Uncle Colton's never scared, I thought. After all, wasn't he a *real* cowboy?

"Well, y-yes," I said, wondering if he thought I was childish.

"Hmph."

Uncle Colton sighed.

"Please call the police," I said. "What if something's happened?"

"Fine. I'll call 'em."

"Thank you, Uncle Colton!" I breathed.

"Yeah, sure. Now go take care of the horses."

I heartily nodded and rushed out of the house to do as he said.

Uncle Colton will fix everything.

* * *

"They're fine," Uncle Colton said gruffly.

Ryker and I stared, waiting for more information.

"Police contacted 'em," he explained. "The truck got broken down, and they were stranded a little while. Got into some other delays, too."

I breathed in relief.

"When will they be home?" I asked.

"Don't know. Probably a few more days."

I sighed in disappointment.

Ryker narrowed his blue eyes.

"Why didn't they call?" he questioned, pushing his western hat up a little higher and then crossing his arms over his chest.

"Don't know," was all Uncle Colton replied.

Sighing deeply, Ryker said, "Thanks anyway."

My brother then walked off.

Uncle Colton turned to me.

"No point in fretting over it," he said. "They'll be back soon enough."

I broke my gaze away from the house and toward the field.

"I suppose so."

"Ya want to go riding?"

Satisfaction washed over me at my uncle's question.

I turned toward Uncle Colton and clasped my hands in delight.

"Oh, yeah!" I breathed.

Truth be told, I had wanted to go horseback riding with my uncle for quite some time.

Uncle Colton smirked a little, and I followed him to the stables.

Of course, I instantly went to get Nightfall. Uncle Colton surprised me by turning toward Blizzard, and I felt a sinking feeling in my stomach.

"R-Ryker doesn't… want you to ride him…" I said, feeling out of place.

"Your brother needs to let loose," Uncle Colton replied. "Always getting riled up about something. Don't tell me you're going to start acting the same way, now!"

I blushed, embarrassed. In the past, I had always looked up to Ryker with admiration. However, Uncle Colton was saying something different, and *he* was a *real* cowboy.

When I didn't answer, Uncle Colton eyed me.

"Well, boy?" he asked. "Don't tell me *you're* going to be all stuck up!"

I didn't want to answer him. And seeing as I was a dunce, and my best friends were just giggling schoolgirls, I worried he thought I was a little lame.

"Well, I…" I began, "I guess it's okay if you ride Blizzard. After all, you're an adult."

Ryker got pretty good grades—they were a lot better than mine, of course—*and* he had lots of cool high-school friends. I had been nervous that once I went to his school, his friends would be a little disappointed upon seeing I wasn't *half* as fascinating as him.

However, Uncle Colton wasn't hugely impressed with Pitchfork.

"I knew ya would come around. Who'd want to be like your brother, anyway? He's *boring,*" Uncle Colton said. "Acts like an old person. And he's bossy."

Bossy? I thought. Ryker was beginning to seem less and less amazing.

Uncle Colton looked at me.

"Are ya going to say something or just stare at me?"

I blushed again, but I couldn't think of how to reply.

Uncle Colton sighed.

"Well, let's get going."

We took the stallions out of the stable, and I remained quiet.

Uncle Colton doesn't think Ryker's anything that great, I thought. *And after all, he used to be a bull rider! Plus, he makes stuff with leather, and I've only ever knitted.*

My uncle seemed quite impressive. Up until then, I had always viewed Ryker in that fashion, too.

We rode a good while, and I allowed the thoughts to slip away, instead enjoying the scenery, the galloping hoofbeats, and the breeze.

* * *

"Say, Uncle Colton," I began, "what was it like being a bull rider in *tons* of rodeos?"

We were riding around the eastern edge of the wheat field.

Perhaps this conversation will help me find evidence for Uncle Colton's innocence! After all, he simply couldn't have cheated in a rodeo.

"Well, it wasn't always easy, boy," Uncle Colton began, "but I won most all that I entered in."

"Cool!" I chirped. "I ride in rodeos every chance I get! Maybe I can be in as many as you've been in one day."

"Maybe. I've seen you got quite a bit of first-place belt buckles."

Excitement swept over me. Uncle Colton was praising my skills! He thought I might have potential!

I was overjoyed to have received my uncle's approval.

"Thanks, Uncle Colton!" I said. "But you should see Ryker's collection; he's got way more."

Uncle Colton narrowed his eyes at the mention of Pitchfork.

"Well, he's been at it longer than you have, anyway," he responded. "You haven't had as long, see."

"But, anyway, tell me more about the rodeos!"

"Well... it's hard work but pleasing. Don't know many more wondrous things than riding a bull."

"That *does* sound exciting," I agreed. "I'd like to try it one day, but I think Mom would get scared that I'd get hurt, you know?"

"Sometimes ya just have to take risks, boy."

I didn't say anything but felt a little admiration toward my uncle.

"Anyway," Uncle Colton began, "lots of people admire ya for your bravery and skill when you're a bull rider."

I listened with interest. After all, it would certainly be fun to be respected.

"Some people, however, don't."

I tilted my head.

Could this be a clue toward Uncle Colton's innocence?

I waited for him to continue.

He cleared his throat. "Some people think you're crazy for trying to ride a bull, and other people..."

"Yeah?" I asked.

"Other people are jealous of ya or something and try to make ya look bad."

That's it!

"I think I may know what you're referring to, Uncle Colton," I said.

"Yeah?"

"Like, I... Well, there's this newspaper, you see, and..." I trailed off, unsure.

"Go on."

"Well... there's this newspaper... It says you

were disqualified from a rodeo—for cheating."

Uncle Colton was not pleased.

"Lies!" he declared. "Where'd you get that?"

"Well, I…"

The girls and I had chosen to keep the bus a secret from the grownups, except Lia's grandmother. While Ryker was aware of its existence, my parents (and Fay's) were not. Lydia, who found the bus in the first place, puts it like this: "The bus is a secret—a treasure—and it's better to keep it that way."

"Well, where'd you get that?" he demanded again.

"Well, um… Lydia f-found it."

"But *where?*"

"I can't tell you."

"Why?"

"Look, Uncle Colton, don't worry about where it was. I knew that it wasn't true, anyway."

"Of course it isn't true!" Uncle Colton shouted. "One of those other rodeo fellas tricked everyone."

I knew Uncle Colton couldn't have cheated… Someone just made him look bad!"

"What should we do?" I asked.

"Nothing, so long as word don't spread across town."

"And if it does?"

Uncle Colton frowned.

"I may have to leave Wilsonville."

BRAWL

Chapter 8

"So, Uncle Colton couldn't have cheated," I explained to Lia and Fay.

Both girls were silent, and that annoyed me.

"See?" I said. "You know he's innocent, now, don't you?"

"Well, I…"

Fay's voice trailed off.

Lydia took a sip of her strawberry milk. We were at the bus, and she had gotten the bright idea to bring a thermos.

"I don't know, Code," she said.

"What do you mean you don't know?" I asked. "There's nothing to *not* understand!"

Lia tossed her hands up in the air, unsure what to

believe, and Felicia cleared her throat.

"Uh, Kodiak, I don't mean for this to sound rude or anything," Fay began, trying to be polite but obviously feeling awkward. "However… just because your uncle *says* he didn't do it, doesn't actually mean he didn't do it."

I took it personally.

"Yeah, well, just because you read something in a *newspaper* doesn't make it true either!" I retorted.

Fay nodded. "Of course. But still, you don't have strong evidence."

"Yeah," Lia agreed and then laughed a little nervously, "I know *all about* not having strong evidence."

"That's different!" I snapped. "You thought someone was *guilty* without evidence; I'm saying someone's *innocent* until there's evidence. If you suspect Uncle Colton, you're making the same mistake twice!"

"But," Fay continued, "it's not that we're against your uncle or falsely accusing him of anything; we just aren't sure *what* to think. So, don't take it the wrong way."

Determined, I rose from where I had been sitting on the bus steps.

"Fine, if you want *more* evidence, I'll *get* more evidence—even if I have to go to Hawaii!"

Lydia let out a small giggle.

"If you're going to Hawaii, maybe you should wait a little while, first. After all, tomorrow's *only* my thirteenth birthday."

Fay smirked and told Lia, "Well, if Cody betrays

you and doesn't show up, at least you'll still have *me*."

I playfully rolled my eyes.

"Of course I'll come," I said. "I love cake almost as much as snickerdoodles."

"That's not the only reason you're coming, is it?" Lydia asked humorously.

"Maybe," I replied. "No, I'm kidding. I'm also coming because there's ice cream."

"Cody!" Fay and Lia yelled, horrified.

"Kidding again," I replied with a snort. After all, Lydia and Felicia were my best friends; I had no intention of ever missing their birthdays.

"What kind of cake is it, Lia?" Fay inquired.

"Strawberry—like this milk," Lydia chirped with a snicker.

I, however, asked a much more important question.

"Well, what flavor is the *icing?*"

Lia grinned at my question.

"It's lemonade-flavored."

"Really?" I asked. "I didn't even know that existed."

"Lia's grandmother always makes lovely cakes," Fay said. "And just think: The cake is going to be *pink!*"

"Unfortunately," I replied.

Both girls yelled in unison, "Kodiak Hugo Nobleman, how dare you!"

I gleefully laughed.

"I'm only *teasing*—though I've never cared much for pink; it's girly."

I'm sure Uncle Colton doesn't like pink, either.

"So, see you tomorrow, then?" Lia asked.

I nodded. "Pitchfork's coming too, of course."

"Cool!" Lia replied.

Felicia gathered up her books. After all, she was determined to study throughout the summer.

"I've got to go home now," she said, "but I'll see you both tomorrow."

"I better leave too," Lia replied, "so, later!"

I waved goodbye to my two best friends and headed home.

* * *

"Your parents called," Uncle Colton said.

Ryker looked up from some random newspaper he was reading.

"What did they say?"

Uriah came walking in and headed to the kitchen, likely going to get himself a glass of water before he went back to work outside.

Uncle Colton glanced at him, and then said, "They're going to be gone a while longer."

"When'd they call?" Ryker asked.

"'Bout fifteen minutes ago."

I perked up.

"Oh, you should have told us then," I replied. "I wish I could've talked to them!"

"Yeah, well... Said to tell you hi... that they missed ya and stuff."

Ryker's dark-blue eyes glared like knives.

"How long till they're back?"

"'Bout three weeks, yeah."

I nodded, but Pitchfork's eyes narrowed.

104

"Why have they been gone so long?" he questioned.

Uriah was sticking around. After all, he was working for Father, so it made sense he was curious.

Uncle Colton shrugged and looked away.

"I don't know."

Taking in a deep breath, Ryker closed his eyes and then set down the newspaper.

"Okay, then," he said. "I'll just have to be patient."

I was disappointed, of course. This had certainly become more than a two-week trip—and it had been so long since I'd talked to Dad and Mom.

Uriah left to a different part of the house, and I decided to go to my beloved wheat field.

Warm sunshine and a gentle breeze greeted me as I opened the door and stepped outside.

It sure does feel nice out here. It's such a shame Dad and Mom won't be back for three weeks!

"Hmm," I mumbled, heading toward the wheat field. "That's about the time of the Fourth of July! Maybe we can buy fireworks and have a fireworks show with Uncle Colton."

I decided I'd ask him later.

I took in the comforts of the wheat field and felt sure it'd yield a very plentiful crop.

I can't wait for Dad and Mom to come back.

* * *

"The cake was delicious, even though it was pink," I chirped. "Thanks for having us over!"

It was June twelfth, Lia's birthday, and Ryker and I were just about to leave her house. However, we were thanking her grandmother first. It was about seven o'clock in the evening, and we needed to get back to the horses.

"Oh, you're welcome," Lydia's grandmother cheerily replied. "I'm glad you could come."

Ryker then started up a conversation with her, and so I ended up tossing a purple balloon around with the girls. Lia's dog, Charity, tried to pop it.

Then we got the idea to add a second balloon to our game, and it wasn't long until a third was added.

"We can't let any of them touch the ground!" Lia screamed. "Hurry—grab that one!"

Fay and I wildly attempted to catch the balloon, but Ryker surprised us all by suddenly diving for it in the middle of his conversation with Lia's grandmother. Much to our relief, he caught it just in time. He then hurled it at Lia and continued his conversation as if nothing had happened.

We continued our game for about thirty minutes. During the game, Charity successfully popped one of the balloons, and *then* my older brother remembered we really did need to be getting back home.

Fay and Lia were going to have a sleepover, so Fay wasn't leaving yet.

We told everyone goodbye and then left Lia's cozy little house. It was significantly smaller than my house—and Fay's—but it was a nice place. It had lots of photos in it, and candles were always glowing. Furthermore, Lia's grandmother was constantly baking something.

"Now Lia's a *teenager*," I said with a snicker.

"You'll be one too next month, Cross Eyes."

"Yeah, like you!"

"Mom might cry," Ryker warned.

I laughed. "Yes, maybe."

We walked a bit faster so it wouldn't be so late once we got home.

I heard a bit of a clatter nearby and turned to see. An alley cat was crawling into a knocked-over trashcan.

Silently, we made our way down the sidewalk. Ryker sighed.

"I just wish Dad and Mom would come back!" he exclaimed.

I nodded in agreement.

"Yeah, me too," I said. "But at least we still have Uncle Colton around."

Ryker fell silent.

I didn't say anything either, instead thinking about how I could get more information to prove Uncle Colton's innocence.

I realized, however, that such would be very difficult since it seemed *everyone* believed him to be guilty.

I probably can't find an article that tells what actually happened.

Still, I was determined to try.

I'll check Father's office when we get inside.

I saw the two-story building come into view, and Ryker and I walked up the driveway. However, Ryker suddenly stopped by the door; all was still.

"Something's not right," he muttered. "You go inside, Cross Eyes; I'm heading to the stables."

My brother walked off to do just that.

"Wait," I said, stopping him in his tracks. "I'm coming with you."

I followed close by my brother, uneasy.

When we reached the stables, Ryker hesitated.

My brother's concerns seemed accurate; there was some loud talking going on in one of the stables.

Suddenly the sound of arguing turned to the noise of a great deal of ruckus.

Ryker darted in, and I followed behind him. What I saw horrified me: Uncle Colton and Uriah Harper were having a brawl!

I was scared half to death. When Uncle Colton fiercely punched Uriah in the shoulder, I couldn't help but gasp. Uriah blocked a couple more attacks as Ryker ran toward the two, yelling in vain to get this brawl to cease. In fact, Ryker got in the way of one of Uncle Colton's punches, resulting in a bloody nose.

In my mind, I couldn't think of a thing to do. It seemed I couldn't run or anything, though I certainly wanted to.

Uriah, in self-defense, landed a rather impressive kick on Uncle Colton's side.

The two men continued to brawl, and when Uncle Colton grabbed a plank of wood, my heart leaped.

Ryker had to think fast; after all, I clearly wasn't going to do any of the thinking at the moment.

Pitchfork lived up to his nickname when he grabbed the nearest thing—a pitchfork. I almost screamed because it seemed Ryker was going to end this fight in a most horrible manner.

To my relief, he did not use the sharp part of the fork but instead turned it to the other side, which was just wood.

With almost lightning speed, Ryker knocked the plank out of Uncle Colton's hands with the wooden end of the pitchfork.

"Stop!" Ryker yelled. "Stop fighting!"

Thankfully, the brawl ended.

Ryker glared at the men, and I quickly handed him a hanky for his bleeding nose.

"What was the point of this madness?" he shouted, his voice shaking some.

Uncle Colton narrowed his blue-hued eyes, and in turn, Ryker narrowed his own.

"Well?" Ryker asked, letting out a shuddering breath. "What was it?"

"None of your business!" Uncle Colton retorted.

Turning to Uriah, my uncle clenched his fists.

"Off this land!" he hollered. "Go."

Taken aback, Uriah responded, "Mr. Honeysett, I *work* here!"

Uncle Colton shook his head.

"Not anymore. You're fired!"

Ryker's jaw dropped.

"You're not *Father,*" he intervened, indignant. "You can't fire him!"

"Well, Ryker Jace," said Uncle Colton firmly, "your father isn't here."

Ryker's nose had stopped bleeding, and he was about to respond, but Uriah cut him off.

"No—I'll leave."

I gasped.

"But Uriah!"

Uncle Colton shot me a look, and I ceased my protest.

Uriah grabbed his western hat, which fell on the ground during his brawl with Colton. Then he left the stable and headed toward the house.

I didn't take a step. Remaining in my spot, I watched my uncle and brother. Currently, they were having some kind of stare down.

It didn't look good.

A few minutes later, I heard Uriah's truck start, and then he was driving off our property.

After that, Uncle Colton saddled up Blizzard and left to go riding, leaving Pitchfork and me in the stable.

My brother had given up on even trying to stop Uncle Colton from riding the horse.

"What's the point?" he mumbled to himself. "It never does good, anyway."

I couldn't reply to the statement and needed to process what all had just happened.

Uriah's... gone!

The thought was obvious, though it had taken time to sink in. He was gone, yes, but... why?

Uriah had always been a hard worker—and he could play basketball—so why had my uncle fired him?

How quickly things had changed! It was only a little while earlier that I had been celebrating Lydia's birthday, and now this?

My brother and I went quietly into the house, and all was a suffocating silence within. In the backyard, the dogs didn't bark, and in the house, Ryker didn't say a word. We were alone. It felt like we had been… like we had been… abandoned.

Dying of thirst, I headed to the kitchen but stopped in my tracks, gasping at a sight.

"Oh, no!" I shouted.

Ryker spun around to my direction.

"What is it?" he exclaimed.

I knelt next to the shattered glass on the ground.

"The picture frame—it's broken!"

"What?"

Indeed, the frame that always held the picture of Ryker and me from years ago was on the floor, cracked.

Ryker heaved a lonely sigh, and his next words were filled with dejection:

"If only Father and Mother would return soon."

Rockets of Fire

Chapter 9

"Get up, Cross Eyes. Come on!"
It was strange. I could hear the voice—recognize it too—but at the same time, I was still asleep.

"Ow! Cody!"

The yelp was undoubtedly from Ryker, and it didn't click with me until later that I must have whacked him in the face with my arm while I was sleeping.

"Well," he began, "if you won't get up, I guess I'll just have to eat all the snickerdoodles…"

To his surprise, I'm sure, it actually took me a

second to spring out of bed even despite his words.
Let's face it: I was tired. Of course, after about five
seconds, the words sunk in, then I jolted up, got
tangled in the covers, almost fell, and then chased
after my brother—who was already running down
the stairs and laughing.

When I reached the floor, however, I stopped in
my tracks.

"Whoa…" I breathed.

In front of me were *loads* of packages of
fireworks!

*How could I have forgotten? It's the Fourth of
July!*

I turned to Ryker.

"Did you buy all these, Pitchfork?"

"No," Ryker replied, "Uncle Colton did, I
guess."

"Sweet!" I chirped. "We get to have a fireworks
show tonight."

Ryker smiled a little at my happiness, but I could
tell he was a little saddened.

"What's the matter?" I inquired.

"They still aren't back."

"I know."

"Uriah's gone, too. Things aren't looking good."

"Maybe Dad and Mom will come back tonight,"
I said encouragingly.

"Maybe."

I went closer to the fireworks.

"Look," I said, changing the subject, "this one's

got a horse on it—it looks like Nightfall!"

Ryker let out a rather small laugh and nodded slightly.

"There's even a solid, pink one."

"I bet that'd be Fay's favorite."

There were fireworks in all different sizes. There were also smoke bombs and sparklers and other little things. It was the biggest pile of fireworks I had ever seen in my life!

I fondly remembered when Ryker and I would go to the fireworks stands with Dad and look at the assortment to choose from. Sometimes Mom would come with us, but other times she would stay home, making snickerdoodles, punch, and homemade ice cream.

"Independence Day is one of my most favorite holidays *ever!*" I chirped.

"Mine too," Ryker agreed.

I got excited just thinking about the holidays I loved to celebrate.

"*And* my birthday is this month!" I yelled in delight, going to open the backdoor so our dogs could come in. I picked up Gopher, and he was thrilled to see me. Blue and Arrow sniffed the fireworks, Blue barking.

I loved all of our dogs equally, but Gopher actually *belonged* to me. He was one of our old neighbors' puppies, and they gave him to me before they moved to Cambridge a couple of years ago. You see, once their puppies were born, I helped take care of them every day; after all, eight puppies were a lot to handle!

And so, Gopher was mine.

So far, evidence proving Uncle Colton's innocence concerning rodeo matters was yet to be found, despite the fact I had been searching. I had checked Dad and Mom's bedroom, the office (though I had gotten distracted while I was in there because, you know, it was time for dinner), and the bus. Still, there was nothing. At the same time, there wasn't any more evidence proving he was *guilty,* so I hadn't given up hope yet.

Perhaps I ought to search the office again since I was distracted last time.

That seemed like a good idea.

* * *

I held my breath.

No one was around. Still cautious, I looked over my shoulder and glanced at the hallway.

The coast is clear. Here goes nothing...

I grabbed the office doorknob, quietly yet quickly turned it, snuck inside, and silently closed the door behind me.

Breathing a sigh of relief, I went over to the file cabinet.

I attempted to open it but failed.

"Humph! It's locked."

Perhaps there's a key somewhere...

I decided to search my father's desk for the key but then ended up carefully examining a stack of papers.

Something's missing—but what?

I *distinctly* remembered the desk looking *different* earlier.

Think, Cody, think! What's out of place?

I examined the papers on top, the family photo, the stack of CD's—all very authentic country music by the way, as Dad has always been fond of such.

The papers! I yelled in my head. *That's it!*

From my memory, I realized clearly that papers which had once been on top were no longer there.

"They've been stolen?" I mumbled to myself, unsure. "Maybe not."

I knew what the papers looked like, but when I had seen them earlier, I hadn't paid much attention to what they said; they were a little over my head, anyway.

I opened up the desk drawers and searched around inside.

They weren't there.

I really wished I had paid more attention to what those papers said!

In the process of my search, I came across a key.

The file cabinet! I thought. *Perhaps I can open it now.*

Thankfully, I was able to unlock the cabinet with ease.

Yanking the first drawer out, I peered inside.

The pile of papers in it wasn't all that high.

It seems like there should be more documents in

here.

I opened the second drawer and gasped.

"Newspapers!" I exclaimed a bit too loudly for comfort. Quickly, I glanced at the door and was relieved that no one burst inside.

Shakily, I picked up the pile of papers. However, I grew disappointed looking through them all.

"How dull," I muttered. "These aren't talking about anything all that interesting."

I put the papers up and checked the third drawer, which contained checks and bills and stuff—as well as a little box. I picked it up, and all that was inside were receipts and a business card.

I was about to put the box back into the third drawer, but I stopped myself and picked up the business card.

It was a business card for some doctor over in Omaha.

What's up with this? I wondered.

I placed the card in my shirt pocket and then put the box back into the drawer.

After I finished my search around the rest of the office, I put the key back in its original drawer.

I was about to exit the office, but when I heard something cringle beneath my foot, I stopped.

A newspaper clipping?

I was pretty sure I hadn't dropped this—which meant someone else did!

Picking it up, I carefully surveyed the small bit of paper.

No!

It was the same newspaper article that Lia found in the abandoned bus, just a different copy.

Which means someone else had this.

I tucked the clipping in my shirt pocket, like I had done with the business card.

I gave the room a quick glance and then snuck out of the office, going up to my room.

* * *

"I think it's going to rain…"

Ryker was right, I realized after looking up at the clouds.

We were outside, next to a plate of snickerdoodles, and were sitting in camping chairs. My family loves to go camping!

It was evening, and Independence Day had fallen on a Sunday this year. We had gotten back from church services a little while ago. Also, a full moon had occurred a couple days earlier, so it was going to be a rather well-lit night.

"What about the fireworks?" I asked, concerned. I was *so* looking forward to seeing the fireworks and hoped the rain wouldn't cause a change of plans.

Pitchfork shrugged. "I don't know."

Selecting a firework, Uncle Colton said, "I'm still going to release 'em. Never been known to miss a Fourth of July."

I perked up.

"What were Fourths of July like for you, when you and Mom were kids?"

Uncle Colton smirked.

"Heather was always getting worried I'd hurt myself, but I sure did love seeing those fireworks 'sploding in the sky."

A look of longing spread over Ryker's face.

"That sounds like Mom," he replied.

"And," Uncle Colton continued, only giving Ryker a quick glance, "my mother always made lemonade and snickerdoodles."

I gasped.

"Snickerdoodles?"

Uncle Colton nodded. "Yeah, recipe's been in the family for years."

I was interested. Not only was Uncle Colton talking about snickerdoodles, but he was also talking about my grandmother. The grandparents on my mom's side live in Mississippi—they have since I was quite young—so I don't see them all that often.

"Everyone loves snickerdoodles," I chirped. "They've always been a hit."

Ryker nodded and quietly said, "Cross Eyes makes them all the time, and if he doesn't, Mom does…"

"How'd ya ever come up with a name like that…?" Uncle Colton asked, referring to my nickname.

I had to snicker, and Ryker only let out a short laugh—he was still uneasy around Uncle Colton.

"It's from a long time ago," I said. I was about to continue when a loud clap of thunder interrupted me.

"Do you think we should cancel the fireworks tonight?" Ryker inquired, looking at the sky with concern.

My heart sank a little, but Uncle Colton shook his head.

"Like I said," he began, "I've never been known to skip fireworks on the Fourth."

Before Pitchfork could reply, Uncle Colton got up and went over a little way from the wheat field, lighting a fuse on a small concrete platform. He took off running toward the house and then watched the fireworks burst in the air.

Blue barked, and Ryker gave him a gentle pat on the head.

"Maybe," started Pitchfork, "Dad and Mom will see the fireworks—if they're nearby."

I grinned and nodded. "Don't give up hope yet, Ryker!"

With contentment, I enjoyed a snickerdoodle—or three—while more fireworks shot up into the air. I could watch those things for hours and not get tired, it seemed, especially if I had cookies nearby.

A gust of wind forced me to push my western hat down more firmly and then grab a fallen sparkler (which wasn't lit) as it started to roll away on the porch.

Ryker got up from his camping chair and went to Uncle Colton, who had just run back from launching another firework.

"Um, Uncle Colton…" he said, "the wind's

picking up, and you're releasing the fireworks a little close to… Maybe we should call it a night."

"Stop trying to spoil our fun, boy!" Uncle Colton retorted, selecting another firework. "I'm going to release them all tonight."

"But Uncle Colton—"

"Didn't ya hear me? I'm launching them *all* tonight!" Uncle Colton interrupted. "Seriously, how do ya live with the guy, Cody?"

I blushed a little.

"We're only having a little bit of fun, Pitchfork," I said meekly. "It'll be all right."

Ryker crossed his arms over his chest, hurt from my subtle betrayal and even more so over Uncle Colton's words.

"Well, I don't think—"

"I don't care what ya think! Just simmer down!" Arrow whined.

Turning on his heel, Ryker came back toward me and dropped into his camping chair.

I watched the next few fireworks but didn't enjoy the event as I had moments earlier. When I turned to my brother's direction, I was surprised to see by the lighting of the fireworks that his dark-blue eyes were watery.

I was shocked. I could only really remember Ryker having tears twice—once when we went to Lia's parents' funeral and once when our old dog, Dusty, died. When Pitchfork had been riding his horse at eleven years old and fell off—resulting in him getting stepped on by Trigger as well as having the wind knocked out of him—or when he broke his foot at the age of nine, he never cried a bit.

All my life I had tried to be like him, but the thing was, I wasn't. We had our similarities, sure, but deep down inside, we were different—because, let's face it, there were so many things he was that I wasn't and that I feared I'd never become.

"Oh, Ryker," I began in sincerity, "I-I didn't mean to... to—"

But I never finished that sentence.

Just at that time, the wind picked up, and one of the worst things I could imagine happened. Uncle Colton had just lit another container, but a strong gust knocked it over. Then, the container rolled and rolled—right to the edge of the wheat field.

It was at that awful moment when it started shooting out its fireworks.

My heart jumped as I saw wheat catch fire. Ryker leaped out of his seat in a flash, but the flames were beginning to spread across the dry crop.

For a moment, I couldn't think. It was as if my brain stopped functioning, and I couldn't think of a thing to do.

Pitchfork ran. He grabbed the nearest hose he could find. Then, it finally occurred to me I should do the same.

I ran, stumbled, then grabbed a hose—twisting the water spout's knob with more force than I thought possible. I tugged the hose toward the wheat field, adrenaline rushing.

The fire was spreading—spreading like crazy!

As the moments flew by, things only seemed to grow worse. The fire spread faster than our hoses could put it out. The flames grew, hot and violent—angry.

The wind didn't put it out but instead encouraged it. Gusts came and made the fire go farther and farther.

We couldn't do it on our own, and Uncle Colton was… gone.

Maybe he went to get help, maybe…

The fire was spreading to the grass—and from there, to the stables.

"The horses!" I shrieked.

I saw Ryker turn to me in the glow of the flames. As the wind picked up, Pitchfork slammed his western hat down on his head with one hand, holding the hose with his other hand.

"Stay here and keep trying to put out the fire; I'm going to try to get the horses!"

Before I could protest, he darted off into the stable that caught fire.

I was scared to death. The fire was spreading; Ryker was in the stable.

Oh, if only it were a nightmare! Then all I'd have to do is wake up.

But I was already awake.

I didn't take my eyes off the stable, instead waiting to see Ryker come out.

He did come out—and with two horses. But then he blitzed back in.

This happened for a few minutes, and all the while, the fire was spreading.

If only the rain would come after all!

Horrified, I saw the stable catch on fire.

We need help! I thought. There was no one, though—Uncle Colton was gone.

Ryker came out with a couple more horses, and then he was zooming back into the stable, despite the fire.

It was only getting worse. The fire was beginning to swiftly consume the stable walls.

Ryker wasn't coming out; I was desperate.

Is everything falling apart?

Suddenly, the stable roof collapsed!

"No…! No, no, no!" I shouted aloud, all alone.

That night was like a terrible bad dream, and yet, it was real.

Thunder and lightning were all around, yet not a drop of rain.

What should I do? I thought in a panic. *If I leave the hose, I can't continue to put out the fire, but at the same time, Ryker's in the stable!*

My mind was going in circles.

The hose slipped from my fingers as I darted toward the stable.

"Ryker!" I screamed. "Ryker!"

I peered into the stable, but I was unsure about venturing in.

All was hot and bright and horrible. Longer and longer the time ticked by, and farther and farther the flames spread.

Where is he in there?

I was so scared.

"Ryker!" I screamed again. "R-Ryker?"

No, no, no... I have to go in there!

At this moment, a part of the wall collapsed completely.

It was all *real*—so very real and so very terrible.

Just as I was about to dart into the stable, not willing to stay outside while my brother was in there, I saw an image from deep inside—moving—running.

Pitchfork!

He ran—ran with his hands full of reins.

When he darted toward the entrance, I reacted quickly and whizzed out of the way.

In haste, my brother came with two horses, jumped the last few feet out of the stable, and landed with a fall on the ground while coughing and gasping.

"Oh, Ryker!" I exclaimed.

"The hose!" he choked out. "We have to put out the fire…"

I held out my hand to him and helped him up with great swiftness. We then darted back to the hoses as he coughed like crazy.

No matter how much water we gushed on the flames, it continued to spread. It was awful.

"It's n-no use!" I gasped. "We'll never put it out."

But then I felt something—something wet from the sky.

Staring up at the clouds, I gasped.

"Rain!"

More moisture fell, and then more. In fact, it turned into a rather intense downpour.

It was a relief to have the rain, but I was continuing to despair; we *still* couldn't put the fire out!

Suddenly, when hope was becoming a distant memory, Ryker yelled, "Cody, look!"

I jerked my head to the direction Ryker was looking and saw someone darting toward us.

I gasped again.

"It's... He's *back!*"

To our immense relief, our trusty hired hand, Uriah Harper, was running toward us!

I could barely believe my eyes, but then it only got better: Another man was coming, followed by another. Help was on the way!

* * *

A half an hour later, I stood outside in the midst of ash and smoke and rain, hugging Uriah as if my life depended on it. I was trying my best to hold back the tears, yet some couldn't be contained.

Uriah was a little taken aback by my somewhat "bone-crushing" hug, but I couldn't help it; I was *so* relieved—and scared.

However, when I saw Ryker coming wearily toward us, I released Uriah and clung to Ryker just about as tightly as I had to our noble hired hand.

"Ow…"

Upon hearing my brother's quiet moan, I quickly let go and stared at him.

"Oh, Ryker! Why didn't you *say* something?" I yelled in horror.

"There wasn't any time, really. The fire had to be put out."

It was no wonder that Pitchfork was in pain; not only did he have multiple cuts, but even worse, his left arm appeared horribly burned!

Adam Bennet, a friend of Uriah's and one of the men that helped put out the fire, came up to Ryker and inspected his arm.

Ryker was grimacing. "How bad is it?"

"Second-degree, I think. I'll take you to the clinic—right now. Where'd you get it?"

"I was in the stable, getting the horses out, when a post fell to the side of me."

The wound looked horrible, and I felt so sorry for my brother.

Uriah cleared his throat. "We'll check to see how the horses are; you guys go see Doctor Layton immediately."

Adam got in his truck and started it, Ryker jumping into the passenger's seat and slamming the door with his good arm. In an instant, they were off.

Uriah and I headed straight to the horses, and Mr.

Blackwood (who was the other man that helped put out the fire) was inspecting Thunder.

"He's got a lot of burns," Mr. Blackwood informed us.

Using a flashlight, I could tell from one look that he was right.

It's horrible!

"How bad is it?" I asked, afraid to know.

"I don't know for sure," Mr. Blackwood replied. "I suppose a vet would be able to know—and help."

Uriah nodded. "I'll try to contact one, then."

I looked away from the horse and over to Uriah.

"Dad's got the phone number for one in Cambridge written somewhere—I think in his office."

"In that case, I'll take a look."

Uriah left, and then I went to inspect the other horses while Mr. Blackwood went to get some wet towels for some of Thunder's more severe-looking burns.

Trigger didn't appear much better than Thunder did. Cupid and Buttercup (two of our other horses) didn't seem to have terrible burns, at least; they were probably first-degree. Nightfall's weren't horrible, but not as good as theirs, either. Thankfully, there were quite a few horses that seemed to be injury free.

As I was observing some of our foals (and feeling very sorry for the injured ones), a thought made its way into my mind, one that was rather important:

Where is Uncle Colton?

I wanted Dad and Mom home more than ever.

At this moment, Uriah came out of the house.

"A vet is coming right now," he said.

Mr. Blackwood sighed in relief.

"That's wonderful."

I nodded in agreement and then said, "But I don't know where Uncle Colton is."

Uriah furrowed his eyebrows.

"That actually leads to a good question: Just how did the fire get started?"

I realized I hadn't filled them in on that part.

"Uncle Colton was letting off fireworks, a-and Ryker was concerned about the weather, but Uncle Colton kept on letting them off, and then the wind tipped one over, and… and… Oh, Uriah, it was just awful!"

I shuddered, partly from the horrid memory and partly because of the rain.

Uriah's hands clenched into fists.

"And why isn't he still here?" he exclaimed, fed up.

"I-I don't know," I stuttered.

Then Uriah said, "Stay here."

Pushing his western hat on more firmly, Uriah spun on his heel and left. I was sure he was going to search for my uncle. Not much time later, he was jumping up into his pickup and driving off into the town.

I headed toward the wheat field—or what was

left of it—by myself. I needed time to think.

Holding my flashlight up to the ruin, the tears returned and stung my eyes.

From what I could see under the light of the almost full moon and with the light of the flashlight, bitter realization finally occurred to me.

How blind I was! I thought with realism. *The wheat field is destroyed, one of our stables is in ruins, and Ryker and our stock have been harmed.*

I didn't try to wipe away the tears. Instead, I welcomed them.

What a reckless person Uncle Colton is! Why did it take me so long to see?

Our crop—our best crop—was burnt to the ground. It was as if Uncle Colton had set fire to dollar bills.

As I stood in the midst of the destruction, I recalled the earlier days—the days when Uncle Colton had just arrived and the wheat field was so golden. Now, he had gone off somewhere, leaving Ryker and me to fend for ourselves, and the wheat field was nothing more than ash.

A slow understanding came to my mind, and I realized with a saddened heart that our relationship had burned to the ground, too.

However, a noise caused me to cease such thoughts for that moment, and I turned my head to the direction of the sound.

I wiped away the tears so that I could see more clearly, and what I saw made me gasp.

I darted away from the wheat field and toward the sight.

"You're *back!*" I shouted, my heart taking a leap and thinking I must be dreaming. "You're back!"

The truck parked and shut off, then the doors flew open. In a moment, I was very relieved and in my mother's arms.

"The wheat field is burned up," I choked out. "And Uncle Colton left."

"What do you mean?" she asked hastily.

Mom released the hug and inspected me as if to make sure I wasn't hurt.

"It's all burned up," I told my parents. "There was a fire, and Uncle Colton left, and I don't know where he is…"

In shock, Dad raised both of his eyebrows.

"Where's Ryker?"

"A-Adam took him to the clinic because his arm got burned…"

Mom gasped.

"How?"

"One of the stables," I said, " caught on fire, and he went to get the horses out."

Then I started to ramble and couldn't stop.

"… And then y-you weren't ever coming home, and Uncle Colton fired Uriah and got mad at Ryker, and then fireworks caught the wheat field on fire, and some of the horses got injured, and, and— everything's a mess!"

I rattled on for a good while longer, telling Dad

and Mom everything.

While I was doing so, a couple pickups came driving in, and I realized they belonged to Adam Bennet and Uriah Harper. What timing!

Adam got out of his truck, followed by Ryker, whose left arm was now all wrapped up.

"Son!" Mom gasped, running toward him. "Oh, how bad is it?"

"Am I-I dreaming, or are you really here?" Ryker asked.

Dad hurried up to my brother.

Ryker gave a slight smile. "You're really here. Oh, I'm so glad…"

At this point, Mr. Blackwood joined us.

Adam cleared his throat.

"I wasn't expecting to see you guys here today. The burn's second-degree, almost third-degree in some parts. Doctor Layton said he was lucky it wasn't any worse."

Dad nodded.

"Thank you, Adam," he said, and then looked at Ryker. "You were brave."

"Oh, Ryker," Mom breathed, "are you all right?"

"Yes, Mother, I am. It hurts, but it's bearable," Pitchfork replied. "Doctor Layton says third-degree burns generally *don't* hurt. That's because the nerve endings are damaged, so I guess it's *good* it *is* painful."

Uriah now got out of his truck and, to my relief (and somewhat surprise), Uncle Colton was with him.

Upon seeing Dad and Mom, Uncle Colton said, clearly sounding annoyed, "Heather? What are you doing back here?"

Mom cleared her throat.

"Colton, I am so *upset.*"

Her voice shook.

"You *left* your nephews after *you* caused a *fire.* I deserve an *explanation.*"

Uncle Colton didn't say anything.

"Colton, please," Mom continued in earnest. "I thought—I thought you put an *end* to your old ways!"

Still, Uncle Colton was silent.

Mom lowered her voice to a whisper, and I could tell she was upset. "I decided to give you a second chance, but you've proved to be just as reckless and irresponsible as ever. I don't know *what* I was thinking. Why… didn't… you… help them?"

Uncle Colton narrowed his eyes.

"What was the point?"

I gasped.

Clenching his fists, Uncle Colton continued. "Someone's always been better than me! Someone could always last on the bull longer, have a more successful ranch, get the job I wanted. It never changes, *never!*"

Mother clasped her hands in earnest. "Tell me *what* that has to do with my sons and my home!"

"My ranch was destroyed, yours was thriving. I

wanted your ranch. Was going to buy it."

"It's not for *sale*," Mom replied. "And still, why would you—would you leave when the ranch you liked was burning to the ground?"

Shivering in the rain, I saw the vet come driving up to help with our horses.

Feeling awkward, Mr. Blackwood excused himself, saying he would go help the vet, and Adam left with him.

Uncle Colton continued: "You've got a big plot of land. I didn't want to grow crops; I wanted to raise livestock. Figured I'd just let the wheat field burn out, and you'd sell 'cause it's your best crop. Then, of course, I'd buy the land and make it my own."

"Well," Ryker began, "more than just the wheat got burnt—like the stable, and my arm."

"Just hush for once!" Uncle Colton replied. "I'm sick of ya. Don't ever want to see ya!"

"Colton!" Mom shouted. "Don't *ever* speak to my son that way again."

Uncle Colton's hands clenched into fists again.

"Be quiet, Heather. *I* was going to take this place. Sure was! But then it had to get all destroyed. Hmph!"

Suddenly, a thought occurred to me.

"Dad, Mom, why'd it take you so long to come back?" I blurted out.

Dad looked at me.

"That's a long story, Kodiak."

Uncle Colton took me even further by surprise when he said, somewhat arrogantly, "It was partly me. *I* kept them away so long!"

"How?" I yelled, feeling angry. "How'd you do it?"

"Had your dad's phone disabled after a while, see? Messed up the engine before they left too."

"Then how did the police contact them like you said when we were worried?" I asked. "You called the police, remember?"

"Didn't," Uncle Colton replied. "That was just to calm ya down. Only *said* I called them."

I was indignant.

"You lied!" I burst out. "Now I see you for all that you are! You aren't who I wanted you to be—a *real* cowboy! I see your cruelty, your selfishness, and your lack of integrity. You may be my uncle, but Uriah's filled that role more than you ever have!"

The words hurt as I said them—they were bitter realizations, cutting my heart into pieces—but oh, they were so very true.

Standing in the rain, Uncle Colton growled under his breath.

"You're just as pathetic as your brother, Kodiak," he said. "I liked you pretty well for a while, but not anymore. I'm sick of ya both!"

Ow.

"You've broken rules and lied. Were you stealing stuff too? I've noticed Mom and Dad's door's been opened a bit at times. What about the papers that vanished from Father's office? Are you a thief?" I inquired, voice loud, my hands curling into fists.

"Don't know what you're talking about!" my uncle replied, his eyes narrowing.

"Do you?" I asked. "Do you?"

"Said I don't know what you're talking about!"

"Then how do you explain their disappearance?" I demanded.

"Never seen them! But *you* have."

My jaw dropped.

"Why would *I* steal Father's papers?" I demanded.

"Maybe 'cause you want me to get in trouble! You don't like me."

I opened my mouth to reply but was cut off.

"Enough!" Uriah shouted. "Colton Honeysett didn't take the papers."

"How do you know?" I questioned. "Did you see someone else take them?"

"He *couldn't* have taken them," Uriah replied, "because *I* did!"

My heart jumped, and Dad's eyes went wide. "Uriah? Explain."

"Wait," Mom said, "Let's get out of this rain." We did so, all heading to the house.

"Well, first off," Uriah began, "shortly after I met Colton, I thought I remembered seeing an article in a newspaper about how someone named Colton Honeysett cheated in a rodeo. Now, he hadn't

136

seemed like a bad person when I met him, but then again, neither did the last person I found guilty, as you all may remember. So, I decided to do some investigating. I had come up with three alternative theories: One, Colton had cheated in the rodeo but had since changed for the better; two, he had cheated in the rodeo and *hadn't* changed for the better; and three, he had been in the rodeo but had not actually cheated, being falsely accused."

I nodded. Uriah always was secretly being a detective!

"I decided to look for evidence, which meant searching *every* bedroom in the house, as well as the office. I also looked for various records in Wilsonville and called several people from Wyoming. I even managed to get ahold of some people that had attended the rodeo that day back in 1995. All my evidence led back to the same basic conclusion: Colton Honeysett had indeed cheated in the rodeo, ruling out the third scenario. And, of course, since he fired me and left the boys to die, the first option is obviously not the case, leaving us with the second one."

I looked at my uncle.

"You said you didn't cheat. I guess that was another one of your lies…"

Ryker furrowed his brow.

"Why did you work so hard on finding out, though? I mean, it was a pretty old ordeal; it's been almost a decade."

Uriah gave a small smile.

"I'm always trying to make sure justice is served."

Uriah Harper was a very admirable person.

He then looked at my father.

"But, Mr. Nobleman, I'm very sorry for searching your house and things without letting you know. You see, I had a tough decision to make. After all, I tried to contact you first, but I didn't have any luck."

Dad nodded. "It's fine."

"But why'd you have to take Father's papers?" I asked.

Uriah smiled. "You see, I was aware it was taking much longer than it should have for Mr. and Mrs. Nobleman to return, so I was concerned. I took some papers about their trip during one of my detective searches. Finding the papers was just a small fraction of the work I did for that exploration."

"Oh," I said. "What about these? Are these yours?"

I pulled the newspaper clipping out of my shirt pocket, as well as the business card.

"I guess I made a mistake," Uriah replied. "I must have accidentally dropped my newspaper clipping. As for the business card, it's not mine."

Dad smiled a little and took the card.

"Actually," he said, "this is mine. It's a business card your mother and I received a very long time ago. It's from the doctor who helped with some complications your mother was having when Ryker was going to be born."

"In that case," I said, "it was a very long time ago."

Now that I think about it, I do remember Dad and Mom saying Ryker was born in Omaha.

This was certainly my most crazy Fourth of July yet.

An End to the Ashes

Chapter 10

It was an early morning, and I was unable to fall back asleep. For a moment, it hadn't occurred to me what day it was. However, when the realization dawned on me, I jumped out of bed.

In an excited whisper, I delightfully announced to myself, "It's July 26…! I'm a *teenager*."

Hopefully Mom won't cry.

A while later, I practically *zoomed* down the stairs, which resulted in me almost falling. I slid into the kitchen as if my socks were ice skates and was quite happy upon the sight of my mother making waffles. At that moment, Dad and Ryker weren't up yet.

"Good morning, Mom!" I chirped. "I'm

thirteen!"

Mom turned around from the waffle iron and beamed once she saw me.

"Oh, Cody!" she exclaimed. "The waffles were going to be a surprise... Well, nonetheless, happy birthday!"

"Thanks! These smell so good, though," I cheerfully replied.

Uncle Colton had left Wilsonville three weeks earlier. As it turned out, he was guilty of more than we had discovered on the Fourth of July. Some of Uriah Harper's fellow undercover buddies had found, upon investigation, that Uncle Colton was actually a rather skilled pickpocket. Such was horrible news; it was a rather miserable feeling, knowing someone I looked up to so much wasn't half as grand as he seemed.

The authorities had taken Uncle Colton, and I didn't know if I would ever see him again. He may be my uncle, but that doesn't change the fact that he needs to be held accountable for his actions.

My whole family was sad, naturally, as to how Uncle Colton turned out, and it was horrible thinking about how Mom must have felt. After all, this was her younger brother!

Anyway, I was pouring myself a glass of milk when I heard someone coming down the stairs. I spun on my heel, eyes falling on my older sibling.

"Well, well, well..." Ryker said with a smirk, "it's my little teenaged brother."

Thankfully, Ryker's arm was better; its burns were almost completely healed, and we were just hoping it wouldn't scar.

"Pitchfork!" I chirped and waved. "Look, Mom's making waffles."

Ryker nodded. "So I see. Happy birthday, Cross Eyes."

I laughed a little. "I'll *never* grow out of that nickname."

"Yep," Ryker agreed. "And that's because you'll always be walking into stable doors."

"And you'll always be Pitchfork because you'll forever be *scrawny* and tall."

"I'm not *scrawny*—I'm just *thin.* There's a difference!"

"Well, you're spindly."

Mom had to laugh at us as she poured some more batter into the waffle iron.

"You're both silly," she said with a smile.

Facing Ryker, I crossed my arms over my chest, pretending to be annoyed. "Well, my eyes weren't even crossed when I ran into the shed wall!"

"Yeah, well, I was tired—couldn't think of the right thing to say."

It was a funny story. You see, a long time ago, when Ryker and I were both quite sleep deprived (we had gone to bed very late, and we had to get up earlier than usual the next day for chores), Ryker had opened up the shed door for us so we could grab some tools. Well, I was an unfortunate three feet too far to the left when I attempted to walk inside—I was half asleep, after all, and not thinking quite clearly. I walked right into the shed door, and it sure did hurt! I pulled myself away, eyes hard to keep open since I was sleepy, and stumbled into the shed. Ryker, not thinking clearly due to his tiredness, called out, "Be careful, Cross Eyes!"—though my eyes were never crossed! We both found his comment funny, and so I've been "Cross Eyes" ever since.

The waffle iron started beeping at about the time Father came down the stairs, and I couldn't help but notice a wrapped present in his arms. It was certainly an interesting shape, and quite a good size! The paper was plaid—also known as tartan—and I was curious.

Dad noticed my watchful eye, and he smirked a little.

"Happy birthday," he said. "I can see you're interested in this."

I laughed. "Yes, I am."

Dad looked at Mom, who smiled gently.

"You might as well just let him open it," she said.

Smirking, Dad handed me the package, and I very carefully opened it—which is unusual for me to do, as I tend to rip open presents immediately.

"Hey, cool!" I chirped. "Just what I've always wanted—bagpipes!"

"Oh *no!*" Ryker yelled, putting his hand to his forehead. "We'll never get any sleep."

I knew my brother was only teasing, so I laughed.

"Yeah, you'll never get any sleep because you'll be so serenaded by my awesome bagpipe skills, you won't *want* to!"

Ryker rolled his eyes in a playful manner.

I turned to Dad and Mom.

"Thanks so much!" I said enthusiastically. "Where'd you get them, though?"

Grinning, Dad said, "That was one of the delays on our trip."

"What do you mean?" I asked.

Mom laughed a little. "We spent two days waiting around on this one small shop to get your bagpipes in from where they shipped them!"

Eyes widened, I exclaimed, "Surely not! You *shouldn't* have."

"It's okay," Mom replied. "Your father and I spent some time with old friends while we waited."

Ryker laughed. "Maybe you should've got Cross Eyes a *kilt,* too."

I rolled my eyes playfully at my brother and blew into the instrument, but, quite frankly, I had no idea how to play it; it didn't sound good at all.

"Once I learn how to make this thing work," I began, "it won't sound like a squealing pig."

Ryker, who had covered his ears, said, "Or it won't sound like how you shriek after I eat the last snickerdoodle."

Mom smirked at Ryker and then looked at me.

"Oh, Cody—how could I forget? Close your eyes and hold out your hands; I have a surprise for you."

I did as she said and felt something heavy, smooth, and round carefully being placed into my hands.

"Open your eyes," my mother told me.

Upon doing so, I let out a gasp in delight.

"A cookie jar!"

Smiling softly, Mom said, "Look inside."

I carefully opened the lid.

"Hey—snickerdoodles!"

* * *

Fay and Lia would be coming over later, much to my joy, though I was meeting up with them at the bus first. (Besides, Mom was intending to make my cake and didn't want me to see it ahead of time.) Currently, I was facing the ash that was once a golden field of wheat. So much had changed—myself included.

I recalled my past folly: how I had viewed my uncle with such wonder and accomplishment. I had to learn the hard way because I had been too blind to accept the truth. What a bitter way that was! Never again would I allow myself to be so willfully blind. Never again would I have such an unhealthy idea of true manliness. Indeed, there's much more to masculinity than just working with leather or riding a bull, and now I was well aware.

I realized my mindset could have been e*ven worse,* and I was glad I woke up from my fantasizing when I did.

Influence is, indeed, a very powerful thing. Yes, it is so strong as to change a person. Certainly, it makes sense to choose who you spend much time with carefully—all it takes is one bad apple to cause the rest in the basket to get nasty.

The lesson was learned. A realization spread over me that said I perhaps didn't *need* to spend time with many kids at school *anyway.* Lia and Fay were certainly good, but what about the others?

The wheat field was burned to the ground. We'd have a financial hardship, no doubt, but I could see a vision of next year's golden wheat. There was hope—hope for the ranch and hope for me. Another relationship wouldn't have to burn like my last one did.

It was as if a warm glow spread over me, thawing out the sadness which still lingered in my heart. Despite the fact I stood amid ash and ruin, I was at peace. Silently, I knew I was a wiser boy than I had been.

"Ahem."

I turned around and saw that my father had come out.

"Oh, hi, Dad!" I chirped.

Dad smiled a half-smile.

"Hey. You've been coming out here a lot recently, looking at all this ash. What's up?"

I blushed a little.

"Oh, it was that obvious? I guess it's been pretty frequent. Anyway, I'm *really* sorry about the wheat, Dad."

"It's not your fault."

"Yeah, well... not *completely,* I guess... But now we've lost *tons* of money!"

"We'll survive."

We were silent for a while longer as I tried to think about how to phrase what I was going to say next.

"Oh, Dad..." I almost whispered.

"Yes?"

"One t-time I… was going to go riding with Uncle Colton, and I… I did something I wouldn't do again."

"What was it?"

"Well, Uncle Colton wanted to ride Blizzard and, um, I felt uneasy about it and tried to talk him out of it a little, but then, I… then I… told him that I supposed it was okay and that he was an adult, after all. But you had *said* to only let Ryker ride him. I-I'm sorry!"

"Oh, Cody…" Dad replied. "I forgive you."

"Thank y-you, Father. I should have told him to just ride another horse. I-I know better now."

"Good," Dad replied with a small smile.

We were then silent again until I said, "But I was thinking… I could… you could… we could… um, s-sell Nightfall, if we have to—to help with all the money we lost because of the fire…"

I hated even saying the words, but it was for a noble cause.

Dad shook his head. "No. We aren't going to do that. I know how much you love that horse, and we aren't going to sell it. Besides, you're entering a rodeo next month, remember? You've got to have a trusty horse for that!"

Dad did have a point.

He grinned. "I'm sure you want to add *another* blue ribbon to your collection."

"Yeah, that's true," I replied with a snicker.

Just thinking about the rodeo got me excited. Friendly competition is great, and of course, so are horses. Count me in!

Anyway, Dad and I chatted some more about various things, and as we did so, we headed to the stables. We had repaired the one that burned down a while ago. Then we went riding and watered the horses—including our new stallion, Blaze, who Father and Mother had bought on their trip.

After that, I (easily) convinced Ryker to go play table tennis with me. We had a lot of fun, even when I accidentally knocked the ball into Ryker's face! Oops.

Once Ryker and I had finished a few matches of table tennis, he and I left the house and went to the bus; we were meeting up with the girls.

Cheerfully, I headed down the sidewalk with my brother, and we chatted with ease about various things, like how big the squashes were getting in the garden, and how Blaze was probably going to be a rodeo champion.

Then we turned into the alley where the beloved bus is.

"Hey, girls!" I chirped. "Guess you beat me to it this time."

Fay smirked. "It's no surprise."

Lightheartedly, I rolled my eyes.

Lia beamed, though. "Happy birthday, Code!"

Fay nodded. "Yeah, happy thirteenth!"

"Thanks!"

Ryker cleared his throat.

"Um hello, girls? I'm here too."

The girls laughed, and Fay said, "Hi, Ryker!"

Lia added, jokingly, "We didn't notice you over there."

Now that we were at the bus yet again, I couldn't help but recall the day Lydia had found the newspaper. That paper had been right all along. If only I had listened!

"This bus is so mysterious… isn't it?" I asked.

The others had to agree, and I, letting out a slight laugh, added, "And just who knows what it'll reveal *next* time there's a mystery?"

Widening her eyes a bit, Fay somewhat shouted, "Next time?"

* * *

Fay and Lia, along with their families, later showed up at the house, of course, because we all liked to hang out, taking any "excuse" we could get, it seemed. My thirteenth birthday was a good enough excuse, I suppose, and so they were all here.

Dad and Mr. Blackwood and Adam Bennet and Uriah Harper (who had been, of course, hired back immediately after Dad and Mom returned home three weeks prior), went into the living room and talked together, while Mom, Mrs. Blackwood, and Lia's grandmother went into the kitchen and chatted away. Ryker, the girls, and I all went off and played video games, however (though Felicia's never been much for such—but Lydia persuaded her easily enough). Sometimes when taking turns on a two-player game, Lia would shriek out to Fay, "No, no, no! Go left! Go left! Hurry—now turn right!" And obviously, Fay was stressed out and under pressure while *I* was at ease because I knew she'd never beat my high score.

After that, we went to play with the dogs. Plus,

Fay and Lia had brought their dogs also, so it proved to be quite chaotic but very fun nonetheless.

Then we had dinner, and after that, I nearly lost it with joy because Mom had managed to bake a snickerdoodle cake! It seemed too good to be true, but it was, indeed, what I thought I saw. She had arranged thirteen candles on top and managed to frost the cake as well.

What a splendid thing it was! And certainly, the snickerdoodle cake was even better with the great company. Naturally, I had half and half dumped over my slice because let's face it: Cake is *amazing* with half and half, and if you haven't tried it with some yet, I don't know what you're waiting for.

That wasn't all. Lydia's grandmother had made the most *fantastic* root beer floats in the *world!* They contained root beer and plenty of ice cream—with quite a large dollop of *molasses* stirred up in each glass. It was deemed the "Molasses Float," and I wasn't complaining! Apparently, Lia and her grandmother invented the recipe one night, and it had proved quite the success!

Suddenly, right after I had finished my slice of cake, the doorbell rang.

"I'll get it," I said, perplexed as I arose and walked to the door.

Peeking through the peephole, I didn't recognize the person.

I opened the door and smiled a little at the man in front of me.

Taking one step forward, he said, "Hello. Are you…? What's your name, lad?"

"Cody."

The man looked a little perplexed.

"What are the names of your family members?"

"Um... why do you want to know that?"

"Well, I... You see, lad, I'm supposed to deliver this package to someone, but I want to make sure it gets to the right person."

"Oh. Well, my dad's name is Nolan Nobleman, and my mom's name is Heather. My brother's name is Ryker."

The man was still perplexed.

"Hmm... I didn't think there *were* people with the last name Nobleman to begin with when I saw the package, but... I guess it must be someone else, because none of those are the names of any person I'm supposed to deliver a package to. I'll keep looking—thanks for your time."

"Sure," I said.

And with that, he turned around, and I was about to close the door when I realized something.

"Sir, wait!" I called out.

He turned around.

"Aye?"

"My *real* name's Kodiak! Cody's just a *nickname*."

The man looked relieved.

"Why, yes! That *is* whom he said to deliver it to."

"He?"

"Oh, yes, Colton Honeysett. You know him, lad?"

"Of *course* I do!" I burst out, shocked. "He's my

uncle."

"Oh, certainly," said the man. "Here's the package."

The package was wrapped in brown paper, like from a paper bag, and it had "Kodiak Nobleman" printed somewhat sloppily on it.

"Thank you for delivering it, sir," I replied.

"Any time," the man responded politely.

He was about to leave again when I stopped him a second time.

"Sir!"

He turned around, just like last time.

"Aye?"

"You look… familiar…"

"I was thinking I saw you somewhere," he agreed.

Then it clicked.

"Hey, you're the man I saw when I was searching for my stallion! Remember? I asked you if you had seen a horse."

"Why, so I do recall! Did you ever reunite with the creature, lad?"

"Yes, I did, thanks. What's your name?"

"Lytle Lennox."

I smiled. "Cool. Well, it was nice to meet you. Thanks for the delivery. And maybe I'll see you again sometime!"

"It was a pleasure meeting you as well."

After I waved goodbye to him, I went into the house and shut the door, walking into the dining room.

"Why, Cody!" Mom exclaimed. "What do you

have there?"

"Um, well, I was just about as surprised as you are, Mom!" I said, taking a seat at the table again. "Somebody delivered this to me from… Uncle Colton."

Lydia's eyebrows shot up.

"Well… that's certainly… interesting."

Mom shrugged and gave Lia a look of agreement.

"I guess you'd better open it," said Mom.

I took a moment to observe the sloppy writing on the paper—and the simple wrapping job as well. I carefully turned the package over in my slightly shaking hands. Horrible memories came back.

Everyone was waiting for me to open it, though, so I did, quietly and carefully opening the wrapping.

Inside was a picture frame—like the one that broke—and a small, torn, note:

> *Sorry about the broken frame.*
> *Was an accident. Got a new one,*
> *though.*
> *—C.H.*
> *P.S. Happy birthday.*

I was a little surprised. At least the broken frame was just an accident, apparently.

"*Oh,*" Felicia breathed, "now you can have that cute picture of you and Ryker in the kitchen again!"

Lia giggled, but I teasingly rolled my eyes and slightly smiled.

"Well…" I said, "at least he fixed one of his

things. That's something good."

In agreement, Dad nodded. "Yes, that's true."

It hurt knowing how bad my uncle had been—all the destruction and sadness he caused. It was a disappointing story, indeed. Even though I had refused to see the signs of danger at first, I eventually saw them clearly and realized that this pain could have been somewhat prevented, had I been wiser. Well, I was determined to never fall into that trap again!

I knew I just couldn't let myself make the same mistake twice.

I'm a different boy now than the one who waited for his uncle's arrival. And... I'm a better boy for it. I'm scratched up but healing, and with the scars as reminders.

With growing happiness in my heart, I realized that I was surrounded by kind, levelheaded people, right then, who wanted what was best for me—and for everyone.

They would help me on my life's journey. I wasn't alone.

And one day, there would be a golden wheat field again. Soon, I would walk out into it and run my hands through it, feeling the warm sunshine and gentle breezes.

There wouldn't be any more ashes.

It's so cool you read my book about Cody! How about leaving a review? ⸚

—Danielle

ABOUT THE AUTHOR

DANIELLE RENEE WALLACE is a teenage author born in Washington State. She established a large love for reading during her elementary school years and a strong love for writing while in middle school. At fourteen, Danielle published her first book, while living in Lubbock, Texas. Her father spent about one year of his boyhood in Wilsonville, Nebraska, the town in which Danielle's series, *Secrets of the Abandoned Bus,* takes place. Currently, she resides in northern Ohio with her parents and two older brothers.

Made in the USA
Monee, IL
21 May 2022

96797847R00100